"Are you all right, Melanie, I mean really all right?"

He asked in a husky voice, his fingertips gently caressing the curve of her cheek. "You've been through a horrifying experience tonight."

A tremor shook Melanie, but she wasn't certain if the trembling was caused by the memory of the brutal attack, or the gentleness of his touch. His eyes gleamed down into hers, the topaz highlights catching and reflecting the golden glow of the fire. For a moment she forgot everything—the threat to her father, the terror she had just passed through, even her promise to help trap Barrymore; nothing mattered.

Nothing save the wild emotion that slowly flooded her body . . .

HER
LADYSHIP'S
MAN

Joan E. Overfield

FAWCETT CREST • NEW YORK

"Do not go gentle into that good night,
Rage, rage against the dying of the light."

—Dylan Thomas

Prologue

London, 1812

"The Earl of Terrington?" Captain Andrew Davies Merrick raised a light brown eyebrow in amazement as he considered what he had just been told. "Surely there must be some mistake, Sir. You cannot possibly suspect his lordship of treason!"

Sir leaned back in his battered chair, his hard blue eyes never leaving Drew's face. "Do you question my evidence, Merrick?" he drawled, his voice deceptively mild.

"Of course not, Sir," Drew answered quickly, his cheeks flushing at the cool censure in the blond man's deep voice. He had been in the spy master's employ for a little over ten months since resigning his commission, and he knew well his superior's mania for accuracy. If he suspected the earl of any wrongdoing, then the case against him had to be very strong. Very strong indeed.

"It is just that I am somewhat taken aback," Drew expanded cautiously. "His lordship has been

1

with the Foreign Service for over twenty years, and there has never been the slightest hint of any impropriety attached to his name."

Sir nodded silently, then cast a wary glance about the smoky taproom where he had arranged to meet Drew. "You were assigned to our diplomatic mission in Alexandria, were you not?" he asked, raising a mug of ale to his lips.

"Yes, Sir. I was quartered there in 1807 prior to joining the general's staff on the peninsula," Drew replied, stretching out his booted feet toward the indifferent fire flickering in the sooty grate. It was late in March, but despite the sharp bite in the wind the innkeeper hadn't seen fit to build other than the most meager of fires. Doubtlessly he was hoping his patrons would seek to warm themselves with strong drink instead, Drew thought, crossing his arms beneath his green redingote.

Sir, as usual, seemed impervious to the cold, looking as warm in his claret velvet jacket and nankins as if he were still in the overheated rooms at Carlton House. "Terrington was also in Alexandria," Sir said, his dark blue eyes resting on Drew's face. "Did the two of you ever meet?"

"No, Sir." A slight smile tilted the edges of Drew's mouth. "I was but a junior lieutenant attached to the mission, and I was seldom invited to join in the festivities at the Embassy. I saw his lordship at a distance a few times, but I am certain he would never recognize me."

Sir reached into his jacket, extracting a folded piece of paper. "I trust you know what this is," he said, handing the paper to Drew.

Drew's hazel eyes widened as he recognized the personal seal of the Foreign Secretary. He unfolded the paper, his face remaining expressionless as he read the missive. "A diplomat ought to have better care of his papers," he commented, handing the set of orders back to Sir. "If this is your proof, I can well understand why you should question his loyalty. May I ask how this came to be in your possession?"

"It was recovered from a French spy we intercepted attempting to slip into Montreal," Sir replied quietly. "Unfortunately he was only a courier, so he could tell us little of the man who gave him the letters. The only thing he would say is that the man was English and that he was attached to the delegation in Washington. I don't think I need tell you of the importance of that mission," he added, a grim expression settling on his aristocratic features.

"Indeed not, Sir," Drew answered, frowning at the thought of what another war with America might mean to the already beleaguered British Army. "And given the contents of that letter, I can well imagine the impact it would have should the information fall into the wrong hands."

"It would be a disaster," Sir agreed with his customary bluntness. "Both for us, and for the men in America hoping to smooth the feathers of the War Hawks. The suggestion of claiming the western portion of the land purchased from France by invading the territory through Mexico was never seriously considered, but there is no way we could convince the Americans of that. War would be inevitable, and the last thing England needs right now is another enemy.

"If Terrington has turned traitor, then it is imperative that we learn how badly the Foreign Service's security has been breached. As you are most familiar with diplomatic protocol, Merrick, I am assigning you the task of ferreting out the truth."

"Very good, Sir," Drew responded, his mind already forming strategies. "When am I to leave for Washington?"

"Actually, you won't have to travel quite that far," Sir told him with a slight smile. "In anticipation of open hostilities, Castlereagh gave orders that all diplomatic personnel traveling with family return to St. James's. The earl and his daughter, Lady Melanie, arrived in England less than a month ago, and they will be coming to London to participate in the season. In fact, 'tis said that the earl means to formally introduce her ladyship to society, as she has never had a season. That is where you will come in."

"Ah, then I take it I am to be the lady's most ardent suitor," Drew drawled, shooting Sir a lazy smile. "If so, then 'tis a mission I undertake most willingly. As I recall, the chit was most comely."

"Do you know her?" Sir asked sharply, his dark blond eyebrows meeting in a worried scowl.

"Not really," Drew admitted, his smile widening as he remembered a diminutive beauty with jet-black hair and eyes the color of amethyst. "As I said, I was a mere junior lieutenant, and as such far beneath her notice. But as I recall, she was a pocket Venus with a sharp mind and an equally sharp tongue, or so rumor would have it. Good Lord," he frowned suddenly, "she must be all of three and twenty now! Rather old to be making her first bows, don't you think?"

"Our information is that she went directly from the schoolroom to being her father's hostess," Sir replied, regarding Drew with interest. "As they have been out of the country for the past five years, there was never time for such nonsense. Not that it matters, of course. What does matter is whether or not the lady may recognize you. Do you think there is any chance, however small, that she would remember you?"

Drew was silent a moment before answering. "I should think it highly unlikely," he said firmly. "Her ladyship had little contact with the regiment, and I am certain we weren't introduced. But even if she did, would it be such a problem? Most men of my age have been in uniform at one time or another, and I think it would make my task of courting her a great deal easier if I could claim a prior acquaintance."

"Yes, but unfortunately the role I have in mind for you is not that of a lover," Sir said, his eyes taking on a teasing glow. "Rather, I want to place you in the earl's household as a servant of sorts. That way you can keep a sharp eye on the comings and goings in the household and even search the house should that become necessary."

"I see," Drew said slowly, digesting what Sir had just told him. "May I ask in what capacity? His secretary?"

Sir shook his head. "Terrington already has a secretary; an assistant, actually. A Mr. Cecil Barrymore, who resides with the earl. No, the position I had in mind for you is that of a butler."

"A butler!" Drew exclaimed, automatically lowering his voice when he sensed the other patrons were glancing in his direction. "Do you mean you wish me to pose as a major domo?"

"Look upon it as a promotion . . . Captain," Sir replied, unable to resist teasing the rather earnest young officer sitting opposite him. "I have thought it all out, and it is the only answer that will serve.

Since Terrington rented out his London home before leaving the country, he will be seeking lodgings for himself and his daughter. With Marchfield's help, the Foreign Secretary will very obligingly offer the earl a lovely home in Mayfair, a home that comes complete with a well-trained staff already in residence.''

Drew shifted restlessly in his chair. The plan had its merits, he admitted reluctantly, and it wouldn't be the first time he had acted a part in service of his country.

"Is there some impediment?" Sir asked, noting Drew's troubled expression. "Are you worried someone else, a visitor to the house, might recognize you?"

"No, Sir," Drew assured his superior. "Like Terrington, I have been out of the country for several years, and I was never one for the social whirl. A younger son of a country squire with no income save his commission isn't exactly considered a welcome addition to the *ton*, you know.''

"Then what is it?"

"Sir, you must know I am only too happy to do whatever my country requires of me," Drew blurted out, his cheeks stained with embarrassed color. "But the truth of the matter is that I fear I am so unacquainted with the duties of a butler, I shall never convince the earl or anyone else that I am a *real* major domo!''

"Is that all?" Sir asked with a wide smile. "You may relax, Merrick. I never send a man into action until he has been most thoroughly trained, I assure you."

"Considering how woefully ignorant I am of such things, I only hope there is enough time to instruct me," Drew grumbled, slumping against his chair.

"I don't know the first thing of what would be expected of me."

"Don't worry," Sir promised softly. "You will."

Chapter One

"I mean it, Papa, I will not do it." Lady Melanie Crawford's dark violet eyes sparked with defiance as she faced her father across the cluttered surface of his desk. "I refuse to be put through my paces as if I were some green schoolgirl fresh from the country!"

"But, my dear, you must remember that in the eyes of society that is precisely what you are," Lord Percy Crawford, the Earl of Terrington, protested gently, regarding Melanie with paternal exasperation. As a seasoned diplomat, he could handle even the most hostile of negotiations with cool aplomb, but attempting to reason with his recalcitrant daughter in one of her tempers was enough to set him quaking in his boots. "You have never been formally presented, after all, and—"

"Stuff!" Melanie interrupted with an inelegant snort, shaking out the skirts of her burgundy cambric gown as she rose to her feet. "I have never heard such fustain in all my life! I've been your hostess for almost five years, Papa; why should I make my bows now? It makes no sense."

"This is society, Melanie, it would go against all laws of nature were it to make sense," the earl replied with a touch of asperity. If only Melanie's disposition were half so pleasing as her appearance, he thought, eyeing his daughter's glossy black curls and creamy rose complexion with resignation. It would have made his life a great deal easier.

He often considered it one of God's more interesting jokes that He should have given Melanie the looks of a pocket Venus and the temperament of a fishwife. Men were drawn to her fragile beauty, only to be sent into full retreat by her waspish tongue and willful ways, and it was little wonder that at three and twenty his beautiful daughter was still unwed, a condition he was determined to change, regardless of the consequences. The way things were going, he wanted the security of knowing Melanie was protected by marriage.

Marshalling his considerable skills as a negotiator, the earl decided to try a new avenue of attack. "I really do not see why you are kicking up such a dust, my child," he said, folding his hands across his ample stomach as he leaned back in his red leather chair. "On the voyage home you seemed quite delighted at the prospect of a London season. Indeed, you talked of little else."

"Yes, but that was when I thought I would be serving as your hostess, and not relegated to some corner with a gaggle of giggling debs," Melanie shot back, refusing to be drawn away from the crux of the discussion by her wily papa's machinations. "As you have often reminded me, Papa, I am no longer in the first blush of youth, and I refuse to make a cake out of myself by pretending otherwise. The very notion of being presented at my advanced age is ludicrous; surely you can see that!"

"I am sure the fact you have been out of the country for most of those years will explain the discrepancy, should anyone be so ill-bred as to make comment," Lord Terrington said in his loftiest voice.

Melanie uttered a heartfelt oath beneath her breath. Papa was right, she brooded. With such an excuse not even Prinny himself would dare to laugh at her. Still, there had to be something she could do to avoid the embarrassment of a presentation at her age. Her well-shaped ebony brows met over her nose as she considered the matter.

"But what will you do for a hostess?" she demanded as inspiration dawned. "It certainly would not do for a diplomat to set up a house without a hostess, and of course *I* could not possibly be presented without some sort of respectable lady to lend me her protection."

"That is so," the earl agreed, delighted that he had already foreseen such a difficulty. "Fortunately your grandmother has kindly consented to join us in London and see that you are properly presented." His light gray eyes took on an amused smile at the chagrin on his daughter's face. "I can see that you are delighted," he added sardonically.

"But Grandmother never leaves her home in the country," Melanie protested, shuddering at the prospect of her coming-out being managed by the dowager Marchioness of Abbington. She dearly loved the elderly lady, but there was no denying Lady Charlotte was anything other than a scheming virago.

"That is so, but then, it's not every day that her only granddaughter is presented at Court," the earl replied with obvious satisfaction, pleased at the easy way he had bested his headstrong daughter. "She is quite delighted, I assure you."

Melanie did not doubt that for a moment. The marchioness had shrieked like a scalded cat when she announced her decision to join her father in Egypt rather than submitting to the rigors of a first season. She had set sail from Plymouth with Lady Charlotte's dire predictions ringing in her ears. Oh, yes, she thought, her lips twisting in a grim smile; she could well imagine her grandmother's delight at finally having her under her thumb.

"I thought we might leave next week." Lord Terrington knew by his daughter's silence that she had abandoned the battle, if only temporarily. "We will need time to settle into the house, and, of course, you and your grandmother will want to visit the dressmaker and arrange your—"

"The house!" Melanie interrupted, turning a victorious smile on her father. "You forget, Papa, you hired out our town house when we left England. Naturally we cannot expect the tenants to vacate merely because we have returned unexpectedly."

"Yes, that would be rather unreasonable of me, would it not?" he agreed, inclining his graying head solemnly. "How fortunate that the Foreign Secretary has been kind enough to offer us an alternative."

"An alternative?" Melanie asked warily, her heart dropping to the toes of her satin slippers as she saw the last avenue of escape closing before her.

"Mmm. It seems the viscount is a friend of the Duke of Marchfield, and when His Grace learned of my difficulty, he very generously offered me the use of his town house for the season."

"How very accommodating of his lordship," Melanie grumbled, reluctantly accepting defeat.

"Yes, it is, is it not?" Lord Terrington asked, a thoughtful note entering his voice. "I'll own I thought it rather odd at the time, considering we have never met. But I gather he did so only to please the Foreign Secretary. For all his racketing ways, His Grace is still a Tory."

Before Melanie could comment, there was a knock at the door, and a well-dressed young man with blond hair cropped à la Brutus entered the room.

"Your lordship, my lady, I trust I am not interfering?" he asked in a deferential tone, his blue eyes moving from the earl to Melanie. "I can come back later if you'd like."

"Not at all, Barrymore, not at all," the earl said heartily, motioning his young assistant forward. "We are almost finished, are we not, my dear?"

"Yes, Papa." Recognizing an evasive tactic when she saw one, Melanie acquiesced nonetheless. Even though her father was nominally on holiday while awaiting a new assignment, a diplomat's work was never done. Each post brought new dispatches from Whitehall, and she knew her father was eager to begin his work. Besides, she admitted ruefully, this would give her the opportunity to retreat in good order rather than to risk complete defeat at her father's hand. Turning to her father's assistant, she gave him a warm smile.

"I trust you won't overtire him, Mr. Barrymore," she said in her soft, musical voice. "He will need to preserve his strength for the delights of London."

"I shall do my best, my lady," Mr. Cecil Barrymore replied, dropping a graceful bow, his eyes never leaving Melanie's face. "And may I say how much I am looking forward to seeing you presented at Court? You will make a beautiful debutante, I am sure."

"Thank you, Mr. Barrymore, that is most kind of you." Melanie managed another smile. She did not know why, but there was something about the handsome man's effusive praise that made her slightly uneasy. He had been in her father's employ since Washington, and although she could not fault his performance, neither could she bring herself to trust him. Shaking off the troubling sensation, she paused long enough to press a kiss on her father's cheek before taking her leave. Her father mentioned leaving at the end of the week, which meant she had fewer than five days to make the necessary arrangements for their move.

At least she wouldn't have to worry about hiring and training a new staff, she thought, making her way to the small study that had been set aside for her use. Although nothing had been said, she assumed the duke's staff would stay on during their brief occupancy. From her previous experience in such matters, she knew the servants would doubtlessly resent her authority, and that she would have to utilize every bit of diplomacy she possessed to keep the house running on a smooth course. It would be difficult, she admitted, but not impossible, and at least there wasn't the barrier of language to overcome. With that thought firmly in mind, she settled behind her desk, dipping her quill in the silver inkwell as she drew up a list of all the things that remained to be done.

"No, no, no, the polish must be rubbed *gently* into the silver, not applied slap-dash as if one were painting a stable!" Halvey, the Duke of Marchfield's butler for the past twenty years scolded, snatching away the polishing cloth from Drew with obvious exasperation. "This fork has been in His Grace's family for fifteen years, and he would not thank you for ruining it. Now again, how do you prepare the mixture for cleaning silver?"

"By mixing Spanish white chalk with ammonia, Mr. Halvey," Drew replied dutifully, wiping a tired hand across his sweaty brow. He and the elderly butler had been locked in the small, airless pantry for what seemed hours, and he was as exhausted as if he'd spent the entire day in the saddle. It was barely seven in the evening, and he had been up since before dawn. How he longed for a respite from the endless training.

"And?" One of Halvey's bushy white eyebrows raised itself haughtily as he glared at Drew.

"And then the silver is rubbed with this." Drew held up a worn leather cloth that had been dipped in rouge.

"Very good." The butler acknowledged Drew's correct answer with a cool nod of his head. "I may also remind you that the silver must be rubbed with a woolen brush before it is repacked, otherwise the patina will be dulled."

"Yes, Mr. Halvey," Drew said, thinking that the formidable butler had missed his calling. He would have made an excellent top sergeant.

"I am sure Captain Merrick will remember your careful instructions, Halvey." A soft voice sounded from the doorway and both men turned to stare at the dark-haired woman who stood there, her dark hazel eyes shining with obvious amusement as she studied them.

"As you say, your grace," Halvey answered, giving the Duchess of Marchfield a stiff bow. "But one can never be too careful. His Grace and Sir did say the captain was to be properly trained, and train him I shall."

"Oh, I have every confidence in you, Halvey," the duchess assured him, casting Drew a teasing wink. "But in the meanwhile, Captain Merrick's presence is requested in the drawing room. You will excuse us, I am sure."

"Of course, Your Grace," the butler said, his gray eyes flicking toward Drew as he rose from his bow. "But see that you are back within the hour, Captain," he instructed in frosty tones. "We will be reviewing the proper manner for discouraging unwanted callers. I fear your air of consequence will require some polishing if you are to be taken for a London butler."

"My congratulations for not laughing, Captain," Jacinda said as they made their way from the servants' hall to the front drawing room. "Not that you would have dared, I suppose. Halvey's air of consequence has never required polishing."

"He is rather overwhelming," Drew agreed, straightening his collar as they walked. "He is even more pompous than one of the royal dukes, and I must admit I am in awe of him."

"So was I when I first came here," Jacinda laughed, recalling her first encounter with the haughty butler. "But Anthony assures me he is the veriest lamb, and I must say he is a major domo par excellence. Prinny has tried hiring him away any number of times, but Halvey will have none of it."

"Loyal to Marchfield, is he?" Drew asked, momentarily diverted at the image of the exceedingly English butler moving stately through the Persian Halls of Brighton.

"Oh, exceedingly, but truth to tell, I suspect Halvey considers the prince beneath his notice. He is an ogre of propriety, you know."

"You must be speaking of Halvey, my love," the Duke of Marchfield drawled, his soft gray eyes resting on Jacinda as they approached the doorway. "You have never forgiven him for criticizing your last novel."

"Well, he called my hero, Lord Stiffback, a fop," Jacinda answered, shooting her handsome husband an impish smile. "But he changed his tune fast enough when I told him *you* were my inspiration for the character."

"Hussy, and after you promised you'd never tell anyone." Ignoring the presence of the other two men, Lord Marchfield bent to deposit a warm kiss on his wife's pert mouth. They had been married for less than a year, and it was obvious to Drew that they were very much in love.

"How is the training progressing?" Sir asked Drew as the Marchfields settled on the settee. "Do you think you will be ready in time?"

"If I don't expire from exhaustion first," Drew replied, easing his muscular frame onto one of the overstuffed chairs set before the fire. "I vow, I had no idea a butler's job could be so demanding. However much you pay Halvey, Your Grace, it cannot possibly be enough."

"That's because you don't know how much I pay him," Anthony remarked, draping his arm possessively about his wife's shoulders. "And I told you, I prefer to be called Anthony, or Marchfield, if you wish to be formal."

"Anthony," Drew said agreeably, thinking the other man was nothing like he had thought he would be. Rumor had it that prior to his marriage the duke was as cold as a marble statue, but wedded life seemed to have softened him. The handsome man with dark hair and ice-colored eyes sitting opposite him was the epitome of the gracious host, but beneath that surface charm was the core of pure steel that was evident in all of Sir's operatives. Drew could well believe he would make the deadliest of opponents.

"My contacts tell me Terrington and his daughter will be in London by the middle of next week," Sir informed them, his blue eyes watching the flickering dance of the flames. "Will that give you and Jacinda enough time to arrange everything?"

"More than enough time," Jacinda answered calmly. "We have already put it about that we plan to spend the season and most of the summer rusticating at Anthony's country seat."

"Do you think anyone will be suspicious?" Sir fingered the fob hanging from his waistcoat. "This is your first season as the Duchess of Marchfield, and people may wonder at your absence."

"Oh, I am sure my 'explanation' will be accepted quickly enough," she murmured, a warm glow making the green in her eyes more prominent. "A lady who is increasing is usually not expected to participate in the social round, you know."

Sir sat up in shock. "Increasing?" he echoed, his eyes going to Jacinda's stomach. "Do you mean you are . . ." His voice trailed off in embarrassment, sending her into a fit of amused laughter.

"Ah, these confirmed bachelors," she said, resting her head on her husband's shoulder. "They are every bit as missish as maiden aunts when it comes to such things. But in answer to your question, Sir, I can promise you that my story can be easily confirmed in about five months should anyone take the trouble to investigate."

"Why didn't you tell me?" Sir demanded, shooting Anthony an indignant look. "I'd never have sent you on that last mission if I'd known!"

"I only learned of it myself," Anthony drawled, placing a protective hand over his wife's abdomen. "The minx refused to tell me sooner because she didn't want me worrying about her and the babe while I was away."

"Well, thank God for that," Sir muttered feelingly, relaxing against his chair. "A distracted agent is worse than useless, and I would never have forgiven myself if anything had happened." There was a brief silence as the three men considered the dangers of their chosen profession.

"The viscount informs me that Terrington has accepted my offer," Anthony said after a few moments. "Apparently he seems to find nothing unusual in my offering my home to a complete stranger. Although I suppose we ought to be grateful; it would have been damned awkward had he refused."

"There was never a chance of that once Castlereagh made the offer," Drew said knowingly. "Terrington is too wily a diplomat to risk offending his exalted superior. I'm sure he was most grateful that the Foreign Secretary should have gone to such pains on his behalf."

"How far is the Foreign Office willing to go with your plot, Sir?" Jacinda asked, casually taking it for granted that she would be numbered among the conspirators. Even though she was a civilian and a woman, she was well aware of the grim necessity for such scheming. As a loyal subject, she was more than willing to do her part for her country, a fact she had already proven with considerable resource-fulness.

"They are being cooperative ... for them," Sir answered with his usual caution. "Although I think they seem overly eager to place a noose about Terrington's neck."

"That means nothing," Drew said, recalling the Corps's fanatical obsession with secrecy. "The slightest hint of anything untoward is enough to send them scrambling for someone on whom they can lay the blame. I'm only surprised it is the earl they are accusing, and not his assistant. It has always been my experience that the higher rank one holds, the less his chances of being accused. The nobility does tend to protect its own when it comes to a scandal."

"An interesting point," Sir agreed, rising to his feet, and crossed the room to the cellarette. "I raised much the same question, and was quickly assured that young Mr. Barrymore was, and I quote, 'above reproach.' Whatever the circumstances of his birth, it would appear he is not without friends. This recommendation came from the highest level."

"What are the circumstances of his birth?" Anthony asked, shaking his head when Sir offered him a glass of brandy. "His name is not familiar to me."

"He is the only son of a country parson and his wife." Drew repeated the information he had carefully uncovered. "She is a distant relation to Lord Marlehope, and one can only assume he is responsible for the lad's present position with the earl."

"Isn't Marlehope the underambassador to Spain?" Sir was frowning as he handed Drew a glass of brandy. "The plan to involve Mexico in any potential war with America originated in Madrid."

"I have already checked on that, Sir," Drew answered quickly. "The duke was in Scotland when the plan was first discussed, and there is no way he could have known of it. Besides, I find it doubtful that he should involve himself in anything unsavory. The man is as ambitious as they come."

"Tell me more of this Lady Melanie," Jacinda demanded with a determinedly cheerful smile. "I overheard Lady Jersey talking, and she said the girl is a bluestocking. How I should love to meet her!"

"You would enjoy meeting any female who has the smallest tinge of blue," her husband told her fondly. "If only to make yourself appear less of a periwinkle."

"Beast." A playful tap was administered to his cheek. "You know I am proud of my mind and my ability to use it. I merely meant that I am happy to know that Lady Melanie is no simpering chit. Perhaps she might prove an unexpected ally should you have need of one, Captain." Bright hazel eyes flashed to Drew.

"An interesting thought, Your Grace," he responded with an easy smile. "But you must know that as his daughter, Lady Melanie must automatically be considered a suspect in the earl's treason. She has moved in diplomatic circles for the past five years, after all, and there is no telling what she may or may not know. Also, it is reasonable to assume she would have some access to her father's papers. Her sex cannot eliminate her as a traitor, you know."

Jacinda colored brightly. "Indeed I do," she said, recalling when she had been accused of a similar crime by Anthony because of the saucy journals she had written as Lady X. That was all in the past, but things had been decidedly uncomfortable for a while. Her generous heart went out immediately to the unknown Lady Melanie.

"Well, I think the poor child is the innocent victim of circumstance!" she declared flatly, her small chin coming up in defiance. "If her father *is* a traitor, then her life will be ruined. Unless you mean to offer the earl one of your infamous 'choices'?" She shot Sir an accusing look.

"The decision is not mine." He answered her question with all due seriousness. "But whatever the outcome, we must be very sure of ourselves before making any accusations. That is why you must be constantly vigilant, Merrick. No one in the house must be considered above suspicion. Not even the servants."

"I have already been looking into that, Sir," Drew was happy to inform him, "but so far I have been unable to uncover anything unusual. The earl's valet is a possible suspect; he has been with Terrington for the past ten years, and has accompanied him all over the world. Lady Melanie's companion is another possibility, although I think we can safely rule her out. She is the daughter of an army major, and my investigation shows she has been with her ladyship for only the past year. It seems her father died unexpectedly, and the woman, a Miss Evingale, was left stranded in America without funds. Lady Melanie somehow heard of her plight and hired her as her companion. I should think it unlikely she would betray her employer."

"I agree," Anthony said, rubbing a thoughtful finger across his bottom lip. Although he was only nominally involved in the mission, he was still eager to offer what help he could. "But what about the other servants? I know diplomatic personnel often employ local domestics when abroad, and given some of Terrington's last postings, it might be prudent to look into their backgrounds."

"I have already done so," Sir told him. "Nothing."

"Then we will have to go on the assumption that the traitor is either Terrington, his assistant, or his daughter," Drew concluded, his lips thinning. "The problem is, how do we prove it?"

"I have some ideas along that line," Sir said enigmatically. "But it may take some time, and time is the one commodity we have precious little of. The Americans are holding debating sessions even as we speak, and a declaration of war is considered imminent. Although the earl has been isolated from any sensitive material, we still have no way of knowing what may have already been passed on."

"You may depend on me, Sir," Drew said fiercely, his hazel eyes flashing with determination. "If the earl or a member of his household has sold us to the French, I will find him out."

"I'm sure you shall, Merrick, I'm sure you shall." A rare smile softened Sir's hard features. "Halvey has assured me you have all the makings of an excellent butler, and as I have already learned to my discomfort, it is almost impossible to keep secrets from one's butler. They are worse than wives when it comes to ferreting out the truth. Just be the best major domo you know how to be, Merrick, and we shall have our answers before the season is half over."

Chapter Two

It was early the following Tuesday before Melanie and her father set out for London. The earl received several urgent missives from Whitehall as they were leaving, and it was decided that he and Mr. Barrymore would travel down in the carriage while Melanie and her companion, Miss Edwina Evingale, followed in the closed barouche. At least, that was the explanation Lord Terrington offered. Privately Melanie thought he had chosen the separate traveling arrangements so that he could avoid Miss Evingale's incessant chatter.

"Are we there yet?" Miss Evingale moaned as the ancient carriage rounded a corner. "I vow my poor nerves cannot take another moment of this dreadful jostling!"

"We are less than an hour from Mayfair, Edwina," Melanie replied, her voice edged with weariness. They had been on the road all afternoon, and her companion's litany of complaints had long since grown wearisome. First the carriage was too drafty, then it was too warm, and now it was the motion of the carriage which affected her. Melanie considered herself as charitable as the next woman, but five straight hours in Miss Evingale's company was enough to try the patience of a saint.

"Close your eyes and think of something else, Edwina," she advised, shooting her pale companion a look of patent long-suffering. "You didn't eat a thing at that last inn when we stopped; perhaps you are simply hungry."

"Pray, Lady Melanie, do not even *mention* food," Miss Evingale pleaded, clutching a handkerchief to her lips. "That awful cook was a murderess, I am sure of it! Just like in *The Plight of Lady Prudence*, where the villainess was the cook in the castle. You remember, my lady, I read it to you on that dreadful voyage from America."

"I remember." Melanie answered glumly, recalling the days she had preferred the storm-washed deck of the ship to the airless cabin she shared with her companion. Miss Evingale had spent most of the time either suffering in the throes of *mal de mer*, or reading aloud from one of her beloved Gothics. The woman was positively addicted to the wretched things, and she had the annoying habit of applying the lurid tales to her everyday life. Although how anyone could go about thinking villains and heroes lurked behind every bush, Melanie was sure she did not know.

"Why don't you tell me about the book now?" she suggested, hoping to distract her from her suffering. "However did a murderess obtain a post as a cook?"

"By employing the cleverest of deceptions," Edwina answered, squeezing her pale blue eyes shut as the coach swayed dangerously. "She pretended to be the orphaned daughter of a constable, but she was actually a dreadful hussy who had designs on Lord Tattleburn. Naturally, both Lady Prudence and I tumbled to her evil scheme at once; imagine hiring a cook who doesn't know the first thing about plucking a fowl!"

"That does seem rather odd," Melanie agreed, rubbing her head with a gloved hand. She prayed they would soon reach their destination, as she was not sure her patience could endure much more.

"Indeed," Miss Evingale responded, delighted at having so attentive an audience. "It was obvious Mrs. Crumbly, that was the hussy's name, by the by, was no mere domestic, but some highborn adventuress who was only pretending to be a servant until she could trick the hero into marrying her. But try telling Lord Tattleburn that! Prudence did, and only look where it got her?"

"Where did it get her?" Melanie enquired dutifully, grateful that her father and Mr. Barrymore were traveling in a separate carriage. Heaven only knew what they would make of so preposterous a conversation.

"The dungeon, of course. He thought she was a madwoman and decided to lock her up." Edwina's sallow cheeks flushed with excitement. "Fortunately the rats were obliging enough to chew through the ropes binding her, and she was able to escape and warn Lord Tattleburn before he ate the poisoned tarts Mrs. Crumbly had prepared."

"I don't see why Lady Prudence bothered," Melanie replied with an indignant sniff. "If any man were to lock *me* in a dungeon, poisoned tarts would be the least of his worries! Well, what became of Mrs. Crumbly?" she asked, intrigued despite herself. "I suppose she soon found herself locked in the cellar with the obliging rodents?"

"Oh, no!" Edwina's eyes flew open. "She forgot about the arsenic she'd placed in the tarts and died an agonizing death! Naturally, Lady Prudence and Lord Tattleburn were married shortly thereafter."

"Naturally. There is nothing like a funeral to bring the romantic out in a fellow," Melanie replied dryly, noting they were within a few blocks of their temporary lodgings.

"Really, my lady, I do wish you weren't quite so cynical." Edwina sighed, eyeing Melanie with gentle reproof. "You have no romance in you, and that is quite unnatural in a girl of your breeding! Why, with your beauty and grace you would make the perfect heroine for one of Mrs. Radcliffe's novels, and I am certain you would never lack for a hero!"

"I thank you for the compliment, Edwina," Melanie said, noting with relief that the carriage was pulling to a halt in front of a large brick house. "But a man who would lock one in the cellar for trying to save his life hardly seems the most eligible of spouses to me, and I would just as lief do without one of the wretched creatures."

"But—"

"No buts, Edwina, my mind is made up," Melanie said as the door opened. "No heroes for me. Even if one does exist, I am convinced we would never suit. Now, come, it is time we were inspecting our new home." With that she accepted the hovering postillion's hand, eager to end their bizarre conversation.

"James, check your cravat, it is crooked," Drew ordered, surveying the footman in front of him with

26

the critical eye of a general preparing his troops for battle.

"Y-yes, Mr. Davies!" the footman stuttered, snapping to attention. "A-as you say, Mr. Davies!"

"Excellent, James," Drew approved, secretly pleased that all of Halvey's careful instructions were now bearing fruit. Given his brief but exhaustive training, he was confident he could pass muster as a butler in even the most exacting of households. Perhaps they might carry this thing off after all, he mused, pausing to flick a piece of lint from another footman's uniform.

"Sorry about that, Mr. Davies," the footman muttered, his cheeks reddening with chagrin.

Drew said nothing, having learned from Halvey that a haughtily raised eyebrow was often more effective than the most blistering of scolds. After inspecting the remaining members of the household, he turned to Mrs. Musgrove, the duke's housekeeper, who hovered anxiously at his side.

"Have the rooms been prepared for the Terringtons and their staff, Mrs. Musgrove?" he asked, straightening his starched cuffs with a flick of the wrist.

"Indeed they have, Mr. Davies," the good woman replied stoutly. Like the rest of Marchfield's servants, she was privy to the deception, and she was eager to do her part for her king and her employer. "I gave Lady Abbington and Lady Melanie the two suites at the front of the house. The earl and his assistant will be put in the Emerald Suite, just as you said."

Drew nodded absently. His choice of rooms for the Terringtons was no idle whim. After studying the lay of the house he had decided it would be best to keep the earl and his daughter as far apart as possible. Even if she wasn't involved in his lordship's treason, it would be easier for him to carry out any reconnoitering he might have to do without having to work around a simpering debutante.

"Very good, Mrs. Musgrove," he said, turning at the sound of a carriage stopping in front of the house. "Be sure to have plenty of hot water waiting, as I am sure Lady Melanie will be wanting to freshen herself after her journey. And mind that you can have tea served in a moment's notice; they may desire refreshment as well."

This inference that she did not know her duties made the housekeeper stiffen with indignation, but she stoically held her tongue. Evidently Halvey had trained him too well, she thought, tucking a strand of graying hair beneath her mobcap. The lad was every bit as pompous as the old tyrant himself!

Unaware of Mrs. Musgrove's thoughts, Drew was busy issuing orders to the footmen. "James, you and William go help with the luggage," he said, peeking through the lace curtains as the postillion leapt down from his perch to open the coach door. "We wouldn't wish to keep our employers standing in that wind, would we?"

"No, Mr. Davies," the footman answered, giving his cravat a final tug before he and his companion went scurrying out the door to carry out their instructions.

"The rest of you take your places," Drew commanded with a snap of his fingers. "I am sure Lady Melanie will want to inspect you once she has rested, but in the meanwhile I want you all on your best behavior. It is imperative that the earl and his family suspect nothing. Is that understood?"

"Yes, Mr. Davies!" they chorused, assuming their positions on either side of the wide front door. Only

Mrs. Musgrove remained at Drew's side, her work-roughened hands twisting nervously in her clean apron.

"This is all so upsetting," she fretted, shooting him a worried look. "Will it go well, do you think?"

Drew stood straighter, feeling the familiar burden of command settling across his broad shoulders. "If I have anything to say in the matter, Mrs. Musgrove, it will," he said, his voice deep with promise as he leaned forward to open the door for the Terringtons.

"Good afternoon, Lord Terrington, Lady Melanie," he said, executing one of the deep bows Halvey had taught him. "I am Davies, His Grace's butler. Allow me to welcome you to Marchfield House."

"Very good, Davies, thank you," the earl said, surrendering his greatcoat, hat, and gloves to Drew. "Hope you have a bit of tea prepared; my daughter and I are quite famished, eh, my dear?" He shot Melanie a questioning look over his shoulder.

"That sounds fine, Papa," Melanie said, giving the butler a cursory smile. She was rather surprised to find him so young and attractive. Her eyes moved past him, noting the apple-cheeked woman with round blue eyes who stood at his shoulder. The housekeeper, she decided, noting the set of keys dangling from the woman's thick waist.

Drew caught the direction of Lady Melanie's gaze, and hastened to perform the necessary introductions. "This is Mrs. Musgrove, my lady," he said, allowing himself to relax slightly when it became obvious that the Terringtons accepted him. "She is the duke's housekeeper, and I am certain she will be happy to assist you in settling in to your new home."

"Indeed I will, my lady." Mrs. Musgrove shot Melanie a look of warm approval. "If you and the other lady will follow me, I shall take you to your rooms."

While the ladies were being shown their new rooms, Drew escorted the earl and his assistant to their quarters. "I took the liberty of placing Mr. Barrymore across from you, in case you might have need of him during the night," he told Terrington, his carefully hooded eyes watching the older man sharply. "I trust this meets with your approval?"

"Yes, Davies, that is fine." Drew was interested to note that it was Barrymore who answered him. "Also, I was wondering if it was possible for a small study to be available for us? Something private, you understand?"

"Of course, Mr. Barrymore," Drew murmured, deciding to put them in the duke's private study. Among its more interesting features was a secret door that would allow him to enter or leave the room unobserved, should the need arise.

He flicked a glance at Terrington, noting the way he kept his dispatch box clutched protectively in his arms. He knew from his days with the Diplomatic Corps that a diplomat was held personally responsible for the papers in his care, and he was intrigued with the care the earl was exercising. Such caution would seem to rule out any possibility that the papers had gone astray through idle carelessness, which meant collusion was definitely involved. He made a mental note to inform his lordship about the hidden safe located in the master suite, a safe to which he, of course, would have a secret key.

The earl had been placed in the largest suite, lavishly decorated in dark green and gold, while Barrymore's rooms were much smaller, and less opulently appointed in shades of pale green and soft yellow. He half expected the younger man to protest such modest accommodations, but to his surprise the assistant seemed well pleased with his new situation.

"Ah, a view of the garden," he said, opening the French windows and stepping out onto the stone balcony that overlooked the back of the house. "How very pleasant. Once the flowers begin blooming, I can leave my windows open and pretend I am in the country. Thank you, Davies." He gave Drew a polite smile.

"You are most welcome, sir." Drew inclined his head in a perfect imitation of Halvey at his regal best. He found the other man's graciousness to be disarming, and was determined not to allow himself to be charmed. Although Barrymore's conduct had more or less been foresworn, he was still too intimately connected with the Terringtons to ignore. If nothing else, he could prove a valuable source of information. With that in mind, he gave him an inquiring look. "Also, sir, I was wondering whether or not you were traveling with a valet? If not, I would be happy to assign one of the footmen to assist you."

"Oh, no, I have my own man," Mr. Barrymore assured him, pausing in front of the mirror to run a hand over his artfully arranged curls. "Indeed, I cannot imagine life without Grisby. He has a sister here in London, and I gave him two days of holiday so that he could visit her."

"That was very kind of you, Mr. Barrymore," Drew said, thinking he would have to run a check on the valet as soon as he was able. "If that will be all, I will be returning to my other duties. Should

31

you wish anything, you have only to ring for the footman." And with that he departed, eager to find out what Mrs. Musgrove had been able to learn of Lady Melanie and her companion.

In her own chambers, Melanie quickly dismissed both Mrs. Musgrove and Miss Evingale, determined to steal a few minutes of uninterrupted peace. After pausing long enough to wash the dust from her hands and face, she began exploring her new surroundings, her delight increasing with each discovery.

The bedchamber was almost twice the size of her rooms at Terrington Court, and a definite improvement over any of the rooms she had lived in during her travels with her father. The furniture was dainty and feminine, carved out of polished fruitwood so rich a color it seemed to glow with golden light. The walls were covered in a delicate shade of blue that was almost silver, a shade that was reflected in the richly woven Aubusson carpets that stretched across the parquet floors. The counterpane on her bed was fashioned out of soft rose moiré satin, matching the heavy drapes that framed the tall windows gracing the far wall. All in all, it was the most beautiful room she had ever seen, and she felt a warm thrill of pleasure that it should be hers, even for so short a time.

When she had delayed the inevitable for as long as she dared, she decided to go in search of Miss Evingale. She found her companion comfortably reclining on a blue and cream flowered chaise longue, her nose already buried in one of her Gothics. When Melanie asked if she would care to go down for tea, the older woman shook her head briskly.

"Oh, no, my lady, I could not bear to look at food just now," she said, her blue eyes wide with dismay. "If you have no objections, I think I shall remain in my rooms and recover my poor strength."

Melanie, who never objected to Miss Evingale's absence, was only too happy to grant her approval. "That might be for the best," she said, giving her a sweetly solicitous smile. "You do look rather pale, now that you mention it. But are you sure you wouldn't like even a small cup of tea? I can send the maid up with a tray."

"Well, perhaps a cup of tea would settle my nerves," Miss Evingale agreed weakly, rubbing a hand across the leather spine of her book. "My lady, may I ask you a question?"

"Certainly, Edwina." Melanie began inching her way toward the door.

"What do you think of Mr. Davies?"

"Mr. Davies?"

"He is rather young to be a butler, don't you think?" the older woman asked eagerly, her eyes beginning to take on a familiar sparkle. "And so very handsome. Such lovely brown hair, and those brooding hazel eyes! He cannot really be the butler, I am sure of it."

Melanie knew she would regret asking, but she felt she had no other choice. "Well, if he's not *really* the butler, then what is he?"

"An impostor!" Miss Evingale replied with dramatic relish, her eyes shining with pleasure.

"Ah, not unlike your friend, Mrs. Crumbly." Melanie had learned long ago that scolding Miss Evingale for her silly fancies only made her cling to them more stubbornly. "We shall have to take care we don't sample any of his fruit tarts while we are here."

"Oh, he's not the villain! One has only to look upon his noble countenance to know that!" Miss

33

Evingale reproved her sternly. "He is a hero if ever I saw one, like dear Lord Fulton in *Lady Pamela's Terror*. You remember, my lady, his villainous uncle seized control of his inheritance and he was forced to act as butler in his own household. I wonder if Mr. Davies has an uncle." She laid a thoughtful finger on her thin lips.

"You shall have to ask him," Melanie said, wondering why she simply didn't dismiss Miss Evingale and be done with it. Certainly no other employer she could think of would tolerate such freakish behavior in a companion, which, she admitted with a disgusted sigh, was precisely why she kept the silly creature on. However would she survive if she turned her off?

Her father and Mr. Barrymore were waiting in the front drawing room which the footman called "The Duchess's Room," and while they discussed the latest news from America, Melanie busied herself pouring their tea.

"It's all a hum, mark my words," the earl said, accepting his cup from Melanie. "The Americans are our brethren, they won't make war on us."

"That is what our fathers thought, and only look where it got them," Mr. Barrymore replied, taking a delicate bite of his cucumber sandwich. "No, the Americans are set on this war, I am certain of it. Had you visited their Congress and listened to the debates, you would know I am right. They are like a pack of angry wolves; they sense the coming battle and they hunger for it."

"That seems a rather odd expression, Mr. Barrymore," Melanie said, shooting him a troubled look from beneath her thick lashes. "How could anyone 'hunger' for a war? From what I have seen, it brings nothing but death and destruction; why should anyone want to bring about something so dreadful?"

"For profit, my lady," Mr. Barrymore expanded, leaning back against the delicately striped chair. "Wars have helped make many a fortune, and the Americans are as eager to line their pockets as any man. And, of course, they have long coveted our western territories. A war would give them the perfect opportunity to seize anything they could."

"But only the War Hawks, Senator Calhoun and his group, are openly hostile toward us," her father protested, his brows knitting in a troubled frown. "The senators from New England are most eager to avoid a conflict, and I know President Madison is not averse to a peaceful resolution. I am hoping to convince Castlereagh to send a new delegation. Although," he admitted with a heavy sigh, "I fear he may not listen."

"I'm afraid I must agree with you, my lord," Mr. Barrymore said with a sad shake of his head. "The viscount must first listen to his own party, and we all know how they feel on the subject of negotiations."

"But another war would be ruinous just now!" Melanie protested, setting her cup down with an angry clatter. "Especially a war which could so easily be avoided. You must not give up, Papa," she said, turning to her father. "You must make them listen to you!"

"Ah, if only I could, my dear, if only I could," the earl murmured unhappily, wondering if he should tell her about the missing documents from his pouch. He had managed to keep the disappearance secret from her, but he knew it was only a matter of time before she learned the truth.

So far the Foreign Office had taken no overt action, but he felt his recall from Washington was caused by more than the Crown's desire to remove nonessential personnel from a potential battleground. For a brief moment he wondered if he ought to take her in his confidence, but in the end he decided against it. Barrymore was right, he brooded, it was best that Melanie remain innocent of the undercurrents around her. For all her sharp tongue and quick mind, she was still only a female, and the less involved she was, the safer she would be.

Chapter Three

Melanie rose early the next morning, eager to assume her domestic responsibilities. Although Lady Charlotte would be acting as her father's hostess, she saw no reason why she should relinquish all authority merely because society had decreed it so. The marchioness wouldn't be arriving for several days yet, and she was determined to have the household well under her thumb before then.

After a hasty breakfast she and Mrs. Musgrove set out to tour the elegant town house. They started in the drawing room where she and her father had taken tea, and when she asked why it was called the Duchess's Room, the housekeeper was happy to explain.

"Well, my lady, 'tis called that in honor of Lady Amanda, the fourth Duchess of Marchfield," Mrs. Musgrove said, a pleased smile on her face as she ran her hand across the back of the gold brocade settee. "She decorated it when she came into this house as a new bride. It was always her favorite room, and when she died the old duke, God bless his soul, refused to change the room by so much as a cushion! The present duke and his lady like it as well; Lady Jacinda receives all of her guests here. She says it's like sitting in a pool of sunlight."

"I can see why she would think that," Melanie replied, giving the yellow and gold room an admiring look. "From the little I have seen, the house is quite lovely. I wonder how they can bear to let strangers stay here, although I am most grateful that they did," she added with a rueful laugh.

"Oh, but this is the first time, my lady," Mrs. Musgrove told her as they turned to leave. "This house has been the Marchfield home for well on seventy years, and none but a Marchfield has ever had the running of it! Why, you could have tipped me over with a feather when His Grace told me he had given you and your good father permission to stay here. And then Mr. Halvey leaving on top of it . . . well, things were at sixes and sevens, I don't mind telling you!"

"Mr. Halvey?" Melanie inquired, stopping to admire one of the portraits adorning the downstairs gallery. "Who is he?"

"Why, he was butler here before Mr. Davies," Mrs. Musgrove said, smugly pleased at how easily she had slipped that bit of information into the conversation. The captain had told them to say he was a recent addition to the staff in the event anyone asked. "Mr. Halvey has been with the duke's family for fifty years, you know, and when he retired, His Grace brought Mr. Davies down from his country house, where he had been the underbutler."

Melanie paused in her inspection of the curio cabinet, a faint frown puckering her forehead when she thought of the young butler. "Then Mr. Davies is new at his position?" she asked, feeling faintly surprised by the information.

"That he is." Mrs. Musgrove nodded eagerly. "He's been with us but a fortnight, and I must say he is settling in nicely. Usually a new butler takes some getting used to, but Mr. Davies fits in as if he had been with us all along. Of course, Mr. Halvey did have the training of him, which probably accounts for it. Although, I still think the lad is a wee bit young," she added confidingly.

"Yes, he is rather young, isn't he?" Melanie said, thinking of Fulford, the butler at Terrington Court. He wasn't a day under seventy, while Davies looked scarce into his thirties. One would think that any servant who had worked his way up to butler would have a few decades on him, she thought, then mentally shrugged her shoulders. So long as he did his job and stayed out of her way, she didn't care if he was still in short pants.

Once they had explored the main floor they went upstairs to the various bedchambers and other rooms. In addition to the suites she and the others were already occupying, there were four sets of rooms, including the master suite, which Mrs. Musgrove explained nervously was always kept locked during the duke's absence.

"I understand perfectly, Mrs. Musgrove," Melanie assured the older woman with a kind smile. "His Grace has already been more than generous by allowing us the use of his lovely home. Although I must own I am rather surprised he and his wife won't be spending the season in town. They are recently married, are they not?" she asked, recalling a piece of gossip she had learned from Mr. Barrymore.

"Not quite a year," Mrs. Musgrove said, looking as pleased as if she had arranged the match herself. "But Her Grace is already increasing, you see, and it wouldn't do for her to stay in the city . . . begging your pardon, my lady."

"Not at all, Mrs. Musgrove," Melanie replied briskly, mentally shaking her head at the foibles of society which dictated an unmarried girl had to be deaf and dumb about even the most basic facts of life. Eager to acquit the housekeeper of any impropriety, she added, "You forget I have spent the past five years traveling with my father, and there is little I do not know of the world. Once one has seen a beggar woman giving birth in the middle of a crowded bazaar, there isn't much left that can shock one."

"My patience me, did you really see such a sight?" Mrs. Musgrove gasped, torn between shock and fascination. "A gently bred girl like you? Whatever could those heathen devils be thinking of?"

"The Egyptians are more matter-of-fact about life and death," Melanie replied, pausing to inspect the hand-painted wallpaper. "And in any case, I don't think the poor woman had much say in the matter. The babe would come regardless of where she was, and there was naught we could do but make her as comfortable as we could."

"*You* helped her?" Mrs. Musgrove's eyes widened in astonishment.

"There was no one else," Melanie said simply, sobering as she recalled the pitiful woman's terror. "A Moslem woman would die sooner than allow a strange man to touch her, and as she had no female relations to help her, there was nothing else I could do. I could hardly walk away and leave her to die."

Mrs. Musgrove shook her head in obvious disapproval, muttering beneath her breath as they continued the tour. They parted company, and Melanie went upstairs to rest until luncheon. As she was going by the study which her father had claimed as his own, she thought she'd stop and wish him good morning. The door was standing slightly open, and without thinking she pushed it open and walked in. Mr. Davies was standing by the desk, and when he sensed her presence he whirled around to face her.

"Good morning, my lady, was there something you wanted?" Drew asked, silently cursing her untimely arrival. He knew he had taken a risk searching the earl's desk, but it was a chance he had felt compelled to take. If the blasted chit hadn't interrupted him, he might have gotten a peek at the contents of the sealed envelope he had found in the top drawer; now it would have to wait.

"No, I was just looking for my father," Melanie said, wondering what he was doing in her father's study. At home, Fulford would never have gone into a room unless summoned. Then she remembered that this was the Duke of Marchfield's home, and that as his employee, Davies was well within the bounds of propriety to keep an eye on things.

"He and Mr. Barrymore are in the library, Lady Melanie," Drew said, skillfully guiding her from the room. "Was there some message you wished to give him? If so, I would be happy to have a footman deliver it for you."

"No, thank you, Davies," she said, unconsciously noting his height and the breadth of his shoulders as she walked beside him. She wondered suddenly if he had ever served in the army, for there was something in the proud way he carried himself that put her in mind of the soldiers that she had met during her travels.

"Did you enjoy your tour of the house, my lady? I trust Mrs. Musgrove answered all your questions?" Drew asked, wishing Halvey had spent more time instructing him in the correct method of discoursing with one's employers. He wasn't even sure if it was proper for him to engage her in conversation, but neither was he certain he could simply walk away without a word.

"Oh, yes, it is a lovely home. You and the staff are to be commended," Melanie said, not seeming to notice his discomfiture. "And Mrs. Musgrove is an exceptional household manager, although I fear I may have given her sensibilities a bit of a shock."

This was hardly the sort of conversation he imagined he should be having, but he was at a loss as to what he should do. He tried imagining how Halvey would respond to the little minx's sally, and immediately one of his dark brown eyebrows rose in haughty inquiry. "Indeed?"

Melanie nodded her head and launched into a quick recitation of what she had already told Mrs. Musgrove. "So you see," she concluded with a laugh, "there was nothing else to be done. The poor woman shrieked at the very notion of a doctor attending her. And once I had actually observed one practicing his art, my sympathies were entirely with her. I know *I* wouldn't want one of them treating me!"

"Yes," Drew agreed, momentarily lost in thought, "the hakims are quite useless, and usually so superstitious that the cures they offer are worse than the disease."

"That is so. I recall once one of our servants was quite ill, and I—" She broke off suddenly, her violet eyes wide as she stared at him. "How did you know that?"

"Know what, my lady?"

"That in Egypt physicians are sometimes called hakims," Melanie answered, recalling her earlier speculations about him. She cocked her head to one side, regarding him with interest. "Have you ever been in Egypt, Davies?"

Drew could cheerfully have bitten off his own tongue, but having spoken the word, he could see no way of recalling it without making Lady Melanie even more suspicious than she already was. Thinking quickly, he allowed a faintly disappointed look to cross his face. "No, my lady, I have never been out of England, unfortunately. It was my cousin, Richard, who had the honor of visiting that ancient land. He was valet to a Captain Briggs, and he accompanied him there. Richard used to write me on occasion, and I recall him mentioning the doctors. He had a very low opinion of their skills; they all but quacked his poor employer to death."

"Oh." It seemed a plausible enough explanation, and Melanie let the matter drop. They continued down the hall, parting company at the top of the stairs.

Thank God he had talked his way out of that trap, Drew thought as he made his way down the stairs. It would seem Lady Melanie was far brighter than he had credited her, and he would have to be very careful to guard his tongue the next time he spoke to her. Not that there would be many such occasions, he reminded himself with relief. As a rule, the lady of the house had very little to do with the butler, a circumstance for which he was highly grateful. It would seem the beauteous Lady Melanie had a decidedly adverse effect upon his mental processes. The less he saw of her, the better.

Luncheon was a quiet affair, the conversation centering on the many changes in London and expectations for the coming season. Miss Evingale had recovered from the journey, and she was as eager as anyone to begin exploring the metropolis. Lord Terrington was unusually quiet, and noting his preoccupation, Melanie set out to tease him out of the doldrums.

"Well, you are certainly dressed bang up to the nines, Papa," she said, her amethyst eyes sparkling with laughter. "Might I ask where you're going looking so dashing?"

"Whitehall," Lord Terrington replied, brightening somewhat at Melanie's words. "Mr. Barrymore and I are hoping to speak to the Foreign Secretary. I still haven't heard about my new post, and I mean to discuss the matter with him personally."

From his position behind the earl's chair, Drew stiffened with interest at the unexpected turn in the conversation. After spending the last hour listening to the most boring of domestic chatter, he had learned little of value, and he was beginning to wonder if Sir had erred in placing him in the household. Apparently he had been too impatient; Sir was always saying it was one of his few faults as an agent. Keeping his expression carefully blank, he moved closer to the table, not wishing to miss a word of what was being said.

"I'm sure there must be some explanation, Papa," Melanie soothed, although privately she had to admit she was beginning to have some troubling doubts of her own. Even though her father had been forced to abandon his last mission through no fault of his own, it could still be read in some circles as a failure. The fact he had yet to be assigned a new post boded ill for them, and she prayed the matter would soon be happily resolved.

"Well, if there is one, I mean to have it," the earl said, his tone grim. "I am not without influence, and I shall use every ounce of it if I must. Even if I cannot see Castlereagh, I am hoping to have a word with Lord Penning, provided he is in," he added, thinking of the many doors which seemed closed to him of late.

"It is interesting you should mention Lord Penning," Mr. Barrymore said suddenly, turning to face the earl. "I have just received a letter from an old schoolmate of mine, a Mr. Frederick Allen. It seems he has recently become His Grace's clerk, and I was hoping to call upon him while we are in London. With your permission, of course." He gave Lord Terrington a diffident smile.

The mention of one of the most powerful men in the admiralty made Drew shift uneasily. The Duke of Penning had access to some highly sensitive material, and he didn't care for the fact that the two men involved in this investigation were planning to visit him. Care would have to be taken to isolate both the duke and this Mr. Allen from anything urgent . . . at least for the immediate future. As Sir was fond of saying, one could never be *too* cautious.

"Certainly, Mr. Barrymore, if that is your wish." The earl bestirred himself enough to offer his assistant a paternal smile. "You mustn't think you need to live in my pocket merely because we are in London. Visit your friend, by all means. After all, you have been out of the country almost as long as we have, and I am certain you must have a great deal to say to each other."

"Indeed we do, my lord," Mr. Barrymore said, looking properly grateful for the earl's generosity. "Indeed we do."

"I'm sorry to be so late, Sir, but I had to wait until the family left for the afternoon before I could slip away." Drew apologized as he joined Sir in his rented rooms. "I hope you haven't been waiting long?"

"Only for about an hour," Sir answered, lounging against the faded cushions of his chair, his sea-blue eyes bright as they rested on Drew's face. "And you needn't apologize, Merrick. I know a servant's hours aren't his own."

"That is so," Drew said with a heartfelt sigh, propping his feet on an ancient hassock. "I have been up since dawn, and it may well be after midnight before I see my bed, especially if the earl should dine out."

"Is that a possibility?"

"Perhaps. He and Barrymore are going to Whitehall this afternoon to seek an appointment with the Foreign Secretary. I gather the earl is getting nervous about Castlereagh's refusal to give him a new post."

"I'll speak to the viscount," Sir said decisively. "We can't afford to arouse Terrington's suspicions, so for the moment we shall have to do our best to keep him happy. What else have you learned?"

"Barrymore has an old friend clerking in Lord Penning's office," Drew replied, pulling a sheet of paper from the pocket of his black serge jacket and handing it to Sir. "Mr. Frederick Allen. Do you recognize the name?"

"No, but I will look into it," Sir promised, pocketing the paper. "We'll send Penning up to his country house in the Cotswold until the matter is resolved, just to be certain. One can never be too—"

"Cautious," Drew finished for him, a faint smile touching his mouth. "That is what I thought you would say. I suppose I should also add that Terrington was planning on calling upon His Grace. Apparently he thinks the duke can intercede with Castlereagh on his behalf. Is there some connection between the two we don't know of?"

"They were neighbors at one time," Sir answered, searching his prodigious memory for the information. "And as is usually the case with the gentry, they are very distantly related. Fifth cousins, if I am not mistaken. But Terrington is deluding himself if he thinks Penning will be of any assistance to him. The Foreign Office and the Admiralty have been at daggers drawn over the Orders in Council for the past five months. Have you anything else to report?"

"Not as much as I would like," Drew admitted, rising to his feet to pace the small drawing room. Like the rest of the suite, the room was poorly furnished in ancient furniture that looked as if it had been salvaged from someone's attic. The humble lodgings befitted Sir's public image as a rake down on his luck, and Drew often wondered how Sir could bear such depressing surroundings.

"The earl guards his dispatch box like an old maid guards her virtue," he expanded, crossing the room to stand before the fire smoking sullenly in the sooty fireplace. "Which means those dispatches couldn't have been taken without his knowledge. Also, while I was supervising the unpacking of his belongings, I noted Barrymore has a wardrobe that would make the prince swoon with envy. Unless

47

the earl pays him a salary that is generous beyond belief, it would seem our young assistant has a private income we haven't uncovered."

"I shouldn't think that possible," Sir said, frowning over the information. "Your investigation was quite thorough, and there was no hint of any money at that time. His wardrobe is extensive, you say?"

"And far above the touch of most assistants," Drew replied, recalling the costly garments that had been placed in the cedar wardrobe. "Coats by Weston, silk pantaloons, and brocade waistcoats in every color imaginable. The fellow is quite the beau. I didn't see any jewelry, but I shouldn't be surprised if he doesn't have a diamond or two tucked away."

"Most interesting, and something well worth further investigation," Sir praised, pouring Drew a cup of coffee from a tarnished but still functional silver pot. "Good work, Captain."

"Thank you, Sir." Drew accepted the chipped china cup, faintly flattered by his commander's words. "Shall I search his rooms once he is settled?"

"Only if you can do so without risk to yourself. Butlers aren't usually found abovestairs, and it might prove awkward for you to be found where you should not be."

"That has already happened," Drew said with a rueful shake of his head, telling Sir how Lady Melanie discovered him in her father's study. "And then to make matters worse, I slipped and used the word hakim in her presence. The next thing I knew she was asking me if I had ever been in Egypt."

"What did you tell her?"

"I spun her some Banbury tale about my cousin

Richard serving as a valet to a captain, and how I had learned the word from him."

"Do you think she believed you?" Sir demanded, some of the tenseness leaving his hard face.

"I think so." Drew shrugged his shoulders uncertainly. "She didn't pursue the matter, at least, and from what I observed of her, had she suspected anything untoward, she would have plagued me to death before letting me go."

"Ah, yes, I recall you mentioning she had a sharp tongue. You also said she was most comely."

"Yes, she is quite lovely," Drew admitted, a vision of Melanie in the lovely gown she had worn at luncheon tugging at his mind. The color had brought out the deep violet of her eyes, and made her skin glow with the richness of cream. He had thought she had looked like an angel or a fairy sprite, and it had taken all of his considerable training as a soldier to keep from staring at her in appreciation.

"Are you attracted to her?" Sir asked in his usual blunt manner.

"Sir!"

"I must know, Merrick." Sir's voice was firm. "Our very lives and the safety of our nation rest upon your carrying out this mission in a successful manner. If there is a chance of your becoming attached to Lady Melanie or of that attachment somehow coloring your judgment, it is important that you tell me now."

Drew's cheeks reddened at Sir's harsh accusation, yet despite his indignation he could understand the need for the question. Espionage was a dangerous, deadly business, with no margin for error. In the field, one agent's life depended upon the judgment of another. Should that judgment become impaired for any reason whatsoever, then that agent had the right to know. If he was in Sir's place, he would have made the very same demand.

"I find her beautiful and charming, although perhaps a trifle too willful for my tastes," he answered, determined to be as honest with Sir as he could. "If her and her father's loyalty were not in question, then I suppose I might be tempted to pay her court. Although I doubt her father would ever accept me," he added, his voice displaying more bitterness than he realized. "As a younger son without prospects, I doubt I would be made welcome."

"Thank you, Andrew," Sir said, using Drew's Christian name. "I appreciate your honesty. And I apologize for pressing you on the matter, but it was necessary, I promise you. I only pray that for your sake, as well as for Lady Melanie's, you will never have to choose between her and your duty. It can be a difficult choice, lad, and a painful one. Believe me," he added softly, his eyes taking on a somber glow, "I know."

Chapter Four

Lady Charlotte Abbington arrived two days later, her ancient traveling coach, drawn by an equally aged team of blacks, creating quite a sensation when it creaked to a halt in front of Marchfield House. Drew had been warned by Lady Melanie that her grandmother was "a trifle eccentric," but this euphemistic description did little justice to the tiny woman in a faded satin polonaise who glared up at him from the doorstep.

"Who the deuce are you?" Lady Charlotte demanded, the hood of her threadbare redingote falling back to reveal a misshapen wig of powdered horsehair.

"I am Davies, my lady," Drew answered, doing his best not to gape at the absurd creature. "I am His Grace's butler."

"Pshaw," Lady Abbington retorted, stepping into the vestibule. "You wasn't butler last time I was here."

"Grandmother, that was back in seventeen

eighty-seven," Melanie chided gently, hurrying forward to rescue Davies from her grandmother's inopportunities. Despite his carefully blank expression, she could tell he was discomfited by the elderly lady's querulous demands. "You really cannot expect the same staff to be on duty after so many years!"

"Why not? *I'm* still here, ain't I?" Lady Charlotte shot back, the violet eyes she had bequeathed her granddaughter snapping with indignation. "It seems to me the least these servants can do is to stay alive. But that's the world for you, no loyalty anywhere." Her attention was next claimed by Miss Evingale, who was cowering by the newel post, regarding Lady Charlotte with wide-eyed apprehension.

"And you are the companion, Miss Evingale, I take it?" she asked, tottering forward to study Miss Evingale through a quizzing glass suspended from a frayed velvet ribbon. "Good," she added at the other woman's wordless nod. "You look just as a companion ought to look: plain as a pikestaff. Are you any good with a needle?"

"Y-yes, Lady Abbington," Miss Evingale stammered, clearly awestruck by the tiny marchioness. "My dear father insisted that I be skilled in all the domestic arts."

"Excellent." Lady Charlotte bared her yellowed teeth in a pleased smile. "I have a gown or two that wants mending; you may see to it."

Melanie opened her mouth to protest this usurpation of her companion, but one glance at Miss Evingale's happy smile stilled her protest. Odd as it sounded, the silly creature looked delighted at having been ordered to perform a task that was usually the providence of a lady's maid. Melanie's eyes flicked toward Davies, who was standing at attention behind them, his expression carefully wooden. Their eyes met briefly, and a look of shared laughter flashed between them.

"Would you like to see your rooms now, my lady?" she asked, turning to her with a loving smile. "I'm sure you must be feeling quite fatigued after your journey." She slipped an arm around the marchioness's waist and began guiding her toward the staircase.

"Nonsense." Lady Charlotte dug in her heels with surprising strength. "I ain't so decrepit that I can't endure a coach trip of four days without sticking my fork in the wall! I want my tea, and then I want to see this great barn of a place your papa has rented for the season. I'm sure he must be paying far too much for it."

"Very good, Grandmother," Melanie agreed with alacrity, her only concern to get the elderly woman safely closeted away before she further disgraced herself. "Tea sounds just the thing; see to it, won't you, Davies?"

Drew waited until they were out of sight before turning to the footman. "You may wipe that smirk off your face, Edward," he rapped out in the forbidding manner of an upperservant correcting an underservant. "Lady Abbington is a guest here, and she will be treated with all due respect. Is that clear?"

"Yes, Mr. Davies!" Edward snapped to attention, the laughter dying from his brown eyes. "But you have to admit the old lady is dashed queer in her upper stories. I'll wager she's an even bigger quiz than the old king himself!"

"With all due respect," Drew repeated, not bothering to answer Edward's rhetorical question.

"Don't forget that for all intents and purposes I am butler here, and that means I can have you dismissed from your post."

The threat made Edward pale with fright. "Yes, Mr. Davies," he said, his expression abruptly serious. "As you say, Mr. Davies."

"Good lad." Drew unbent enough to favor the young footman with a warm smile. "Now kindly inform Mrs. Musgrove she is to prepare a tea tray for our guests. I shall see that the marchioness's bags are taken to her rooms."

"Yes, sir!" Edward gave Drew a tenuous smile, then rushed off to carry out his instructions.

After Edward departed, Drew turned to the other footmen, noting from their rigidly held faces that further warnings were unnecessary. He ordered them to carry the bags upstairs, then left to have a word with the marchioness's coachman. Marchfield House did have a small stable around back, but the earl's carriage and team, along with Marchfield's curricle and team of bays, were already stabled there. Accommodations for Lady Charlotte's rig would have to be made elsewhere.

He also decided to do his best to avoid Lady Abbington. He knew of her visit to Marchfield House, of course, but it had never occurred to him that she would remember the staff. The threat she posed to the carefully orchestrated deception was a small one, but it was a threat he felt he could not ignore. As with Lady Melanie, he would give the marchioness a wide berth, and if that did not work, he would have to see what plans Sir might have. With matters coming to a crisis point, he dared not leave anything to chance, not even a dotty old woman.

While Drew was off seeing to his duties, Melanie

was kept busy trying to keep her grandmother from redesigning the Duchess's Room.

"Well, I don't see why you're setting up such a hue and cry." Lady Charlotte pouted when Melanie told her somewhat sharply that she could not have the room repainted during her stay. "After all, I am a marchioness, and while I am in residence oughtn't the room to be called the Marchioness's Room? Besides, I detest yellow." She gave the walls an angry glare.

"Perhaps so," Melanie agreed with studied patience, "but the fact remains that this *is* the Marchfields' home, and I do not think they would thank us if we were to take to repainting the walls after they were kind enough to let us stay here."

"Pooh, people who let out their houses to perfect strangers are made of sterner stuff than that," Lady Charlotte said, lifting up the lid of a Dresden box and peering inside. "Although it's all dashed queer, if you ask me. I've never known a Marchfield to do anything for anybody unless there was a profit in it for them. Or unless it was in the line of duty. The Marchfields have always had a stern sense of duty." She slipped the small box into the reticule dangling from her voluminous skirts.

"Then I am sure that accounts for it." Melanie calmly rescued the small treasure from her grandmother's purse and returned it to the table. "Papa said the duke offered his home only after he had spoken to Lord Castlereagh."

"I wish we might have met the duke," Miss Evingale volunteered with a loud sigh, her blue eyes glowing with pleasure as she studied the small portrait of the duke and his bride that adorned another table. "I vow he is a most handsome man."

"His grandfather was quite dashing, too," Lady

Charlotte said, a smile of remembrance touching her pursed lips. "Black hair, and eyes as cool and clear as diamonds. Ah, well"—she shook off the memory—"no use mooning over the pair of them; one's dead, and the other's married off. What we must do now is concentrate on finding a husband for you, Melanie. Admittedly, you're rather long in the tooth for a deb, but I'll be hanged if I'll let you whither into an old maid." Her eyes flashed toward Miss Evingale, who simpered with delight at the marchioness's scarcely veiled insult.

"You mustn't concern yourself with me, ma'am," Melanie said, all of her incipient resentment at her uncertain position rising to the fore. "I have no wish for a husband, I assure you."

"Of course you don't." Lady Charlotte gave her a sagacious look. "The wretched creatures are usually more bother than they are worth, but still they have their uses. Now, since you are an earl's daughter and an heiress in your own right, I don't think we should settle for anything less than a viscount. But the first order of business will be a trip to the dressmaker. You surely do not expect to go out in society dressed like *that*."

Melanie glanced down at her round dress of green muslin. It was in the first stare of fashion, or so the modiste she had engaged had told her. And it was a great deal more presentable than the moldering gown adorning her grandmother's back, she thought, struggling to hold on to her temper.

"Your concern is most touching, Grandmother," she began coolly, "but as I have already been to the dressmaker, there is nothing left to be said."

"Is there not?" Lady Charlotte sniffed, eyeing Melanie's gown with obvious disdain. "That rag might do well enough for some chit fresh from the schoolroom, but it makes you look a perfect cake. You're three and twenty, Melanie, and that is far too old to go about dressing like a gel."

So much for sparing her grandmother's tender feelings, Melanie thought, her jaw clenching with anger.

"We'll go to Bond Street," Lady Charlotte decided, ignoring her granddaughter's flashing eyes. "With the season not three weeks away, we've not a moment to lose! Order our carriage, and we shall leave at once!"

Watching her grandmother shop put Melanie in mind of a conquering army on the march; she swept all before her. Having wormed the name of the most sought-after modiste in London from the daughter of an old friend, Lady Charlotte swept into the salon demanding the attention she felt befitted a lady of her rank and advanced years.

"But of course the young lady must have a new wardrobe," the seamstress, a Madame Philippe, gushed, her almost black eyes moving over Melanie with patent eagerness. "And I quite agree with my lady that the insipid fashions of the young girls will not do. We shall design a whole new look for her, *quois*? I shall give the matter my personal attention."

"Of course you shall," Lady Charlotte said, clearly expecting no other answer. "We shall start first with the dress she will wear for her presentation at Court. It must be white, of course, but I want it to look like something a grown woman would wear." She settled back in her chair while Madame and her assistants rushed about to do her bidding.

Melanie spent the next several hours standing in sullen silence while various swatches of fabrics in a rainbow of colors were held against her for her grandmother's approval. Despite the excesses in her own dress, Lady Charlotte possessed a fine clothing sense, and Melanie had to concede that many of the fabrics and patterns she picked out were the same she would have chosen had she any say in the matter.

"I still don't see why I must be presented," she muttered as she was jabbed with yet another pin. "With the king so ill, it hardly seems the proper thing to do."

"Goose." Lady Charlotte gave a derisive snort. "If the *ton* won't let that tiresome little Corsican interfere with the season, whyever should they let a trifle like a mad king stop them? Besides, it is to Queen Charlotte and Prinny you will be making your bows. Actually, I think we ought to be grateful it is poor King George who has lost his reason. Only think of the difficulties if it had been the queen? You would be forced to be presented to that loose-living Caroline, and a fine farce that would have been!" She gave a delicate shudder. "We might as lief introduce you to a Covent Garden abbess!"

After hearing that treasonous bit of speech, Melanie kept her lips firmly sealed, not even objecting when her grandmother ordered up a dozen new silk gowns in the most stunning shades. Finally Lady Charlotte had had enough, and ordered Madame to have the gowns delivered by the end of the month.

Once their business with Madame Philippe was complete, the marchioness ordered the coachman to drive them to Ackerman's Repository on Oxford Street. The large emporium, which occupied several buildings, had opened a few years earlier, and Lady Charlotte was eager to explore its many delights. Even Miss Evingale, who usually detested

58

shopping, expressed a desire to visit the famous arcade, an interest which was easily explained when she began speaking of all the titles said to be available.

"What sort of books?" Lady Charlotte demanded, bending a suspicious frown on the other woman. "Not improving books? I can't abide the prosy things. If I want to know what God thinks, I shall ask Him when I see Him."

"Oh, I'm sure they have some of those," Miss Evingale said, her loud sniff letting her opinion of that form of literature be known. "But as it happens, I was referring to *real* books, my lady—novels."

"Can't say as I've ever read a novel," Lady Charlotte confessed, relaxing against the soft velvet squabs of the coach and readjusting her wig. "But so long as they ain't dull as ditchwater, I suppose it wouldn't hurt to buy a dozen or so of the things."

Ackerman's was filled with customers in search of bargains, and while her grandmother and companion perused the ceiling-to-floor bookshelves, Melanie drifted over to a counter to inspect some fine Indian silks newly arrived from Calcutta. She was about to ask the clerk for the price of a particularly lovely paisley shawl when she was accidentally jostled from behind. She turned around, the apology she had been about to utter dying on her lips as she recognized the other woman.

"Mrs. Mason, what a delight to see you!" she cried, extending a gloved hand in welcome. "I trust you and your family are well?"

But rather than returning Melanie's warm greeting, the older woman drew back, her dark eyes snapping with dislike as she glared at her. "Well!" she exclaimed, her round face purpling in anger. " 'Tis a fine thing when decent people are accosted in public by the likes of you! I quite wonder that you should have the brass to even show your face!"

Melanie's cheeks flamed at such rude treatment. She had met the Masons in Washington, where the older woman's husband had been employed by the Foreign Office, and the two families had shared the same ship on the return to England. She had never cared for the woman and her encroaching manners, but she had always treated her with cordial respect, a courtesy Mrs. Mason was obviously not willing to accord to her.

Aware that the woman's strident voice was attracting an unwelcome amount of attention, Melanie decided to stage a strategic retreat. "I am sure I have no notion what you mean, Mrs. Mason," she said, her small chin coming up proudly. "I was but offering you a civil good day; my apologies if I have intruded." And she turned and walked away, her lips tightening at the buzzing whispers that followed her.

She found her grandmother and companion still poring over titles, and tersely informed them she had a headache and wished to leave. Miss Evingale was instantly solicitous, slipping a comforting arm about Melanie's shoulders and guiding her out the door. Even her grandmother seemed concerned, her violet eyes thoughtful as they took in Melanie's glittering eyes and slightly flushed cheeks.

"You are looking a bit feverish," she declared once they were safely settled in the carriage. "I shall have Cook prepare you a purgative once we are home."

Melanie was silent on the brief journey to Mayfair, her initial anger slowly giving way to confusion. Whatever did Mrs. Mason mean by her preposterous accusations, she brooded, her expression faintly troubled as she studied the flow of carriages and horses moving past their window. It was obvious that she had meant every word she had spoken, for the animosity emanating from her had been quite genuine. But why should she hate her so? What had she or, indeed, any member of her family done to deserve such rancor? That was the question for which there seemed to be no answer.

Over the next two weeks Melanie was kept too busy to brood over Mrs. Mason's cryptic remarks. At first she'd considered telling her father of the incident, but in the end she decided against it. Papa was highly protective of her, and she didn't want him taking out his anger on the malicious woman's poor husband. Besides, no one of importance had witnessed the incident, and she thought it best to let the matter drop.

Another reason she hesitated confiding in her father was that he seemed so distracted of late. His appointment from Castlereagh had finally come through, but rather than being assigned a new post abroad, he had been given a position as a liaison between the Foreign Office and the Cabinet. He had an impressive title, he told Melanie with a sad smile, but that was all that could be said of the appointment.

Lady Charlotte had settled into the household, and she and Miss Evingale had grown as close as two inkleweavers. They spent hours closeted away in the marchioness's rooms reading the latest offering from the Minervian Press, and Melanie discovered she now had two determined romantics plaguing her.

"I think Edwina has the right of it," Lady Charlotte declared one afternoon as they were sitting down to tea. "That Davies is as handsome as any of our other heroes. Can't imagine why he insists upon posing as a butler."

"Perhaps because he is a butler," Melanie replied resignedly, thinking she really had to do something to control Miss Evingale's vivid imagination. This wasn't the first time she had taken such a fanciful notion into her head. In Washington she had developed the notion that Mr. Barrymore was really the long-lost son of a nobleman, and she'd spent several weeks mooning over the embarrassed assistant until Melanie was forced to speak sharply to her.

"Hmph." The marchioness gave a loud snort as she helped herself to the cream cakes. "As if I ever saw a butler that was as tanned as a native! If you wish to claim ignorance, I suppose there is nothing I can do about it. But do not think I shall not say I told you so when he is proven to be a duke or some such thing."

There was an uncomfortable silence as the others devoted their attention to their plates. Melanie thought she detected a gentle twinkle in her papa's gray eyes, while Mr. Barrymore's brows were puckered in a frown. Doubtlessly he was remembering Miss Evingale's foolish accusations, she thought, and gave him an encouraging smile.

"And how are you enjoying London, Mr. Barrymore?" she asked encouragingly, hoping to set him at his ease. "Were you able to visit with your friend Mr. Allen?"

"Only briefly, I fear," he answered, shooting her a grateful smile. "We seemed destined never to be in the city at the same time for more than a few days. I had barely unpacked my bag before he and Lord Penning set out for the country. But I was able to spend a quiet evening with him at his club before he left."

"Yes, I had heard Penning had left the city," the earl said, nibbling on a piece of Mrs. Musgrove's sherry cake. "And rather odd I thought it, too, given the messages out of Washington. With war imminent, one would think the P.M. would want him close at hand. Ah, well"—he shrugged his shoulders—"as I have discovered, there is no understanding the workings of the government."

"Are matters so grave, then?" Mr. Barrymore asked, his expression troubled. He was dressed in a new jacket of blue velvet and a pair of cream-colored pantaloons, and he looked every inch the English gentleman.

"I fear so, although I hear little gossip closeted away as I am," Lord Terrington admitted with a heavy sigh. "But from what I have heard, it seems Parliament will be considering a declaration of war by the end of the debating session."

This talk of war silenced even the irrepressible Lady Charlotte, as they considered the hardships another war would bring. After a few moments had passed in silent reflection, Melanie stirred herself to ask about the vouchers for Almacks which had arrived that morning.

"Are you quite certain it is all right for me to attend?" she asked, setting her teacup aside. "I won't be presented until next week, you know."

"Of course it's all right!" Lady Charlotte fairly bristled with indignation. "I am the Marchioness of Abbington, and if my name is not enough to lend you countenance, there is your own title to be thought of. I should like to hear anyone, even that baggage Sal Jersey, say one word against you!"

"Actually, it was Lady Jersey who helped secure

Melanie's voucher," the earl pointed out with his usual diplomacy. "Although I am sure she did so only to oblige the prince."

"Yes, the world knows how obliging Sal can be when it comes to Prinny," Lady Charlotte sniped with malicious pleasure. "One may only wonder what this world is coming to when two such notorious females as Sally Jersey and Lady Hertford set themselves up in judgment of others."

"Lady Abbington!" The earl regarded his mother-in-law with horror. "I pray you will keep such talk to yourself! I would not wish my daughter to suffer for your vicious tongue."

"Pooh, when all the *ton* knows those two possess the morals of a Jezebel," the marchioness grumbled, stuffing another cake into her mouth. "But I suppose you are right; 'tis best not to say aloud what one may think privately. Heaven knows it would take only the merest breath of a scandal to ruin a girl's chances."

"I have also received a voucher for Almacks," Mr. Barrymore volunteered unexpectedly. "My mother's distant relation, Lord Marlehope, was kind enough to secure one on my behalf, and I must own I am a trifle nervous."

"Nonsense," Melanie said briskly, thinking how closely his trepidations mirrored her own uncertain feelings. "I have seen you at several Embassy functions, and you have always carried yourself well. You will do fine, I am sure."

The talk soon turned to the upcoming season, and while her father and Lady Charlotte exchanged remembrances of past seasons, Melanie fell into a contemplative silence. She had been telling the truth when she had praised Mr. Barrymore, she realized, studying the amber depths of her tea. The man possessed the skills and charm of a seasoned diplomat, and his blond good looks and noble bearing gave him the air of a true aristocrat. In America he had often been mistaken for a member of the nobility, a misapprehension she noted he was always quick to correct.

She smiled slightly, remembering his mortification when he heard the fairy tales Miss Evingale had been spinning about him. He had been red-faced with embarrassment as he denied any knowledge of what she was talking about, and she had believed him at once. But looking at him now, she found herself wondering if perhaps there wasn't the smallest bit of truth in Miss Evingale's accusations. A moment later she was shaking her head in gentle disgust.

What on earth ailed her, she wondered, relieved no one was privy to her foolish musings. Evidently all this talk of heroes and secret identities was beginning to affect her reason. Next she would be thinking Davies the victim of a scheming uncle, she decided, taking care to hide her amusement as she turned her attention back to the conversation at hand.

Chapter Five

"For heaven's sake, child, will you please stop squirming?" Lady Charlotte snapped as she painstakingly pinned the sparkling aigrette atop Melanie's jet-black hair. "However am I to get this wretched thing on straight with you hopping about like a flea? Now, hold still!"

"I am sorry, Grandmother," Melanie said, doing her best to sit quietly as the marchioness finished her self-appointed task. "But I am so nervous, I am not certain I can stay still. Are you quite certain this gown is acceptable?"

"For the hundredth time, yes," Lady Charlotte mumbled around a mouthful of hairpins. "You look quite dashing in it, too, so kindly stop quibbling. You told me yourself you had no desire to look like an aging schoolgirl, and I can assure you that in that gown there is no possibility anyone shall mistake you for a mere deb."

That was so, Melanie thought, studying her reflection with a worried frown. The gown was white, as was the custom set by the patronesses at Almacks, but there all similarity to the gowns usually worn by debutantes ended. Fashioned out of silk, the gown clung lovingly to her curves, displaying her femininity in a manner which Melanie found faintly shocking. The rounded neckline exposed her neck and shoulders, and was cut low enough so that the gentle swell of her breasts was clearly visible.

She turned slightly, and the hundreds of sparkling rhinestones which had been carefully sewn to the bodice and slim skirts exploded into a dazzling display of pure fire. A ribbon with more rhinestones attached to it tied beneath her breasts, giving the impression she was dressed in a shower of diamonds. Even the aigrette in her hair was ablaze with rhinestones, and Melanie knew she had never looked lovelier. Perhaps, she brooded, nervously fingering the skirts of her gown, society would not be as horrible as she had feared it would be.

"There." Lady Charlotte stepped back, eyeing her granddaughter with pride. "You look like a fairy princess. I vow there won't be a man there tonight who won't fancy himself madly in love with you!"

"Thank you, my lady," Melanie said, turning to give her grandmother an impulsive hug. "May I say you are also looking quite attractive? That is a new gown, is it not?" She studied the fashionable ball gown of black satin with relief. She had been secretly fearing her grandmother would appear at Almacks in one of the gowns she had brought with her from the country and which had been out of fashion for more than fifty years.

"Edwina made me wear it," Lady Charlotte replied with a childish pout. "She said it was just what Lady Catherine might wear. Do you like it?"

"It is quite fetching," Melanie assured her, not asking who Lady Catherine might be. Her grandmother had developed Miss Evingale's habit of mistaking the characters in their beloved novels for real flesh and blood people. Lady Catherine was doubtlessly some heroine out of one of the books they devoured with such glee. "I also approve of your turban, ma'am. Most dashing."

"That was my idea." Lady Charlotte reached up to give the white plume adorning her black turban a loving pat. "I decided my wigs looked odd without those lovely polonaises, and I must own it is far more comfortable. Perhaps I shall wear them more often."

"That might be wise," Melanie approved, guiding her grandmother from the room and down the stairs to where the others were waiting for them. "And another new gown wouldn't go amiss either," she added, images of weaning her eccentric grandmother from her outmoded wardrobe tugging at her mind.

Both her father and Mr. Barrymore were loud in their praises of her new gown, and there were tears in her father's eyes as he pressed a kiss to her gloved hand.

"If only your beloved mother were alive to see you tonight, my dearest," he said, gazing upon her with loving pride. "I have never seen you looking so lovely."

"Thank you, Papa." Melanie blinked back tears of her own, deeply touched by her father's words. Her eyes drifted over to Davies, who was standing beside her maid, her cape of deep purple velvet draped across his arm. Although his face was carefully devoid of any expression, she thought she detected a flash of masculine appreciation in his hazel eyes, and she turned quickly away.

"I am in agreement with your father, my lady," Mr. Barrymore said, giving Melanie a low bow. "You are indeed a vision to behold. Those amethysts are new, are they not?"

"Yes, a gift from my grandmother to celebrate my first evening at Almacks," Melanie answered, rubbing a finger across the chain of glowing purple stones that circled her neck. A small circlet of amethysts and diamonds was clasped around her slender wrist, while two large teardrop stones dangled from her ears.

"May I presume upon your good graces and bespeak a dance, my lady?" Mr. Barrymore continued, his blue eyes filled with admiration. "I dare say your card will be instantly filled once the other men catch a glimpse of you."

"I should enjoy that, Mr. Barrymore," she answered with a genuine smile. Despite the disparity in their ranks, she had never looked down upon Mr. Barrymore, and often danced with him in Washington. He was not a graceful dancer, but he was at least an adequate one, which was more than could be said about the other partners she had been forced to endure in the name of diplomacy. "May I be so bold as to remark that both you and Papa are looking quite handsome?"

"Thank you, my lady." Mr. Barrymore's chest swelled with visible pride. Both he and the earl were dressed in black velvet evening coats and white silk breeches, their starched cravats tied with precision. Her father wore one of his many citations pinned to his jacket, and a large gold signet ring adorned his finger. Mr. Barrymore wore no jewelry at all, save for a small diamond winking from the

69

folds of his snowy cravat, but still he managed to look a trifle more elegant than her father. But then, she realized with a flash of insight, he often did.

Since Lady Charlotte was Melanie's chaperone it was decided they could dispense with Miss Evingale's services for the evening, a decision her companion greeted with amazing tolerance. She wished them a pleasant good evening, and after adding her gushing words of praise to the others', she went skipping up the stairs, an ever-present Gothic clutched protectively to her bosom.

As there was just the four of them, it was decided they would take the duke's carriage, and all too soon they were pulling up before the sacred portals of Almacks. Standing in the line which was forming on the carpet walkway in front of the famous club, Melanie felt a wave of uncertainty wash over her.

What if society didn't like her, she brooded, nervously wetting her lips with the tip of her tongue. What if she did not take? She wouldn't care so much for herself, but she couldn't bear the thought of disappointing her father. He seemed so concerned she should do well.

"Ready, my dear?" the earl asked, laying a protective hand on her bare arm.

Melanie gave him a quick smile, firmly pushing her disquieting fears aside. She covered his hand with hers, giving it a loving squeeze. "Ready, Papa," she said softly, her small chin raising with unconscious dignity as they began climbing the wide marble staircase leading to the Assembly Rooms.

"Are you quite certain you wouldn't like a cup of punch, Lady Melanie?" Sir Christopher Whitney asked for the third time in as many minutes, his gray eyes studying her face with puppylike adoration. "I would be more than happy to fetch it for you!"

"Well, perhaps a small cup," Melanie relented, more out of a desire to be shed of her eager suitor's presence than out of any real thirst for the sickly sweet orgeat which was the only refreshment offered by the patronesses. "Thank you, Sir Christopher."

"I won't be but a moment," he promised, his eyes taking on the fanatical glow of a young Galahad about to set out in search of the Holy Grail. "Wait for me here."

After he departed, charging his way through the crowd like a Hussar, Melanie drifted over to the corner, where her grandmother was holding court on the Dowager's Bench. Shortly after her name had been called out by the club's major domo, the marchioness had settled down for a coz with her oldest and dearest friends, her duty apparently complete as far as she was concerned. When she saw Melanie standing before her she shot her an angry scowl.

"And pray why are you wasting time standing here?" she demanded, lowering her voice to a low rumble. "You won't catch yourself a beau by hanging about me. Off with you now." She gestured toward the center of the room with her fan.

"My apologies, Grandmother." Melanie refused to be cowed by Lady Charlotte's less than cordial welcome. "I came only to see how you were doing, and whether or not you required anything to drink. It's monstrously hot in here."

"I am doing fine, thank you, and should I require anything, I am more than capable of having one of

the footmen fetch it for me," the marchioness informed her querulously. "Now, hurry back to your
young buck before that hussy Amanda Cummings
succeeds in taking him away from you. She's been
casting cow eyes at him all evening!"

Melanie glanced over one slim shoulder, her eyes
colliding with a pair of dark brown eyes sparkling
with obvious malevolence. The younger girl's rather
large nose came up haughtily, and she turned away
with a toss of her brown curls. "If she wants Sir
Christopher that badly, she is more than welcome
to him as far as I am concerned," Melanie replied,
turning back to her grandmother with an amused
smile. "He is much too young for me."

"He's a good three years older than you, *and* the
heir to a comfortable estate in Kent," Lady Charlotte informed her snappishly. "You could do better, I admit, but you could also do worse. Now, get
back to him before that vixen snatches him away
from you."

"Yes, my lady." Melanie knew her grandmother
too well to waste her time in useless debate. She
returned to the alcove where Sir Christopher had
left her before setting out on his quest. A small
settee had been placed there next to several drooping palms, and she sat down with a grateful sigh.
She had been dancing for several hours, and her
slippers were beginning to pinch her feet. Deciding
she would be more comfortable if she loosened them
a bit, she bent down and began unlacing the ribbons.

". . . true, then?" A woman's voice came drifting
from the other side of the potted palms. "How simply shocking! Is Jarvis quite certain? Cedric is a
member of the Privy Council, and he's not heard a
word of this, I am sure. He tells me *everything*."

She stressed the last word heavily, indicating it would not go well for the unknown Cedric were he to do otherwise.

"Oh, yes." A second woman began speaking, her voice fairly dripping with malicious delight. "I heard him telling Lord Thorne that 'tis the talk of Whitehall!"

Melanie's ears pricked up at the mention of the Foreign Office. Papa hadn't mentioned anything about a scandal, she thought, surreptitiously scooting to the other side of the settee so that she could eavesdrop with greater comfort. This was so exciting, she mused with a sudden flash of irreverence, just like those silly Gothics her grandmother and Miss Evingale were forever reading. All it lacked was a swooning heroine and a dark-eyed, mysterious hero!

"Well, 'tis his daughter I am sorry for," the first woman said with a heavy sigh. "Poor child, I suppose she will be ruined once the scandal is known?"

"Quite ruined," the other woman answered with relish. "She will most certainly have to retire from society, and naturally marriage is out of the question. What gentleman would want to join his name to the daughter of such a man? Such a pity, really, for she is very beautiful."

Ah, there was the heroine, Melanie thought, her eyes sparkling with silent laughter. Perhaps if she waited long enough, the hero of the unfolding drama would also make himself known. She leaned closer, hoping to learn more.

"Will he be arrested, do you think?" The first woman was speaking, making no effort to hide her eager interest. "He deserves it, and to be hung, too, if even half the talk is true! Imagine, one of our very own selling us out to the French! It quite makes one wonder what is becoming of our world."

Melanie's amusement with the conversation vanished at this whispered comment. It was one thing to laugh over a potential scandal involving cards or a ladybird, but it was quite another when the safety of the nation was at risk. The other woman had mentioned Whitehall; surely she could not be implying that a diplomat had betrayed his own country, she brooded, appalled at the very thought. She would have to tell Papa at once.

"Oh, he will swing, I am sure of it, once they have the evidence they need." Melanie heard the women's skirts rustling as the two rose to their feet. When she next heard them, their voices were fading as they moved away from the alcove. "They have already recalled him from Washington and it won't be long until he is clapped in irons. Poor Lady Melanie, one may only wonder what will become of her then."

"Here you are, my lady." Sir Christopher appeared before her, a cup of punch in his hand. "I am sorry to have been so long, but Lady Jersey wished to speak with me, and you know what she is like once . . . my heavens, Lady Melanie, are you quite all right? You are as pale as a ghost!"

"I—I am fine, Sir Christopher," Melanie managed to say, her shaking voice and pale cheeks giving lie to her assurances. "I am just a trifle overheated."

"Yes, it is as hot as the very devil in here," he agreed vaguely, thinking that her face was rather white for one claiming to be suffering from the heat. Still, a gentleman never questioned a lady's word. Then, as if just remembering the cup in his hand, he thrust it at her. "Here, you must drink some of this," he urged, spilling some of the contents onto her skirts. "I am sure it will help."

Melanie stared down at the milky beverage, trying to control the wave of nausea that washed over her. Calling upon her inner strength, she raised the cup to her lips and forced down a small swallow. God above, she thought, struggling to control her emotions, whatever was she going to do? Someone was accusing her father of treason!

"It went quite well, don't you think?" Lady Charlotte asked some three hours later as the carriage wended its way home. "With any luck we shall have you safely leg-shackled within a fortnight, m'girl."

"Yes, Grandmother," Melanie replied dully, her eyes closing as she laid her throbbing head on the back of the carriage. The preceding hours were all a blur to her, and she had no idea what she had said, or to whom she had said it. She knew she had danced, and smiled, but her actions were those of a sleepwalker caught up in the most horrific of nightmares from which there was no escape.

"The Earl of Clarebourne seemed particularly taken with you," Lady Charlotte prattled on, not seeming to notice her granddaughter's odd silence. "Although I did think it was rather fast of you to stand up with him for two waltzes, Melanie. You must have better care of your reputation."

A vague recollection of a plump, red-faced man in a yellow waistcoat flashed briefly in Melanie's mind. She remembered him bowing in front of her and asking for permission to lead her out, but that was all. "Yes, Grandmother," she repeated, turning sightless eyes toward the window.

"Are you feeling quite the thing, my dear?" her father asked worriedly, leaning forward to study her in the faint light of the flickering torch. "You've scarce said a word all evening."

Melanie blinked back sudden tears at his concern. Dearest Papa, she thought, love welling up inside her. Did he have any idea of the evil rumors being spread about him? "I am fine, sir," she said, her voice husky with emotion. "I am just feeling overwhelmed by everything, that is all."

"Nonsense." He gave her a hearty smile. "Why, I have seen you charm a roomful of diplomats without turning so much as a hair! Are you sure there is something you're not telling your papa?"

"Indeed not, sir!" she denied hastily, stunned by his acuity. "It is just as I told you—London society is much different than what we are used to, and I am having a difficult time finding my feet."

"Well, if you are certain." The earl was clearly not convinced. "But I shouldn't worry, my dear. I heard the young men talking, and all are bowled over by your beauty."

"Thank you, Papa," Melanie replied, swallowing painfully. She was torn with the desire to cast herself into his arms and sob out what she had heard. But she could not in front of the others. She trusted Mr. Barrymore's discretion, but she was too familiar with her grandmother's quick temper and equally quick tongue to think she could remain silent in the face of the rumors that were being circulated.

"Well there, you see?" He gave her chilled hand a loving pat. "It will all work out, never you fear."

"If you say so, Papa," Melanie said, a single tear escaping from the corner of her eye and trickling down the curve of her cheek. "If you say so."

Drew had waited up, as befitted a proper butler, and he held the door open for the Terringtons as they entered. "Good evening, my lord," he said, relieving the earl of his black silk evening cape. "I trust all is well?"

"Quite well, Davies, quite well," Lord Terrington replied jovially, handing his cane and gloves to the hovering footman. "Were there any messages from Whitehall for me while we were away?"

"No, my lord," Drew answered, wondering what sort of message the earl had been expecting.

"Ah, well, I thought not," the older man replied as if in answer to Drew's unspoken question. "Still, one never knows. Well, Mr. Barrymore, what was your impression of Almacks? You have been almost as quiet on the subject as my daughter."

"Most interesting, my lord," Mr. Barrymore responded, running a hand through his thick blond hair. "It was a great honor to see so many of our illustrious citizens assembled together. I must own to being somewhat awestruck by it all."

"A good answer, Mr. Barrymore," the earl laughed in approval. "'Tis obvious you shall go far in your chosen career with so diplomatic a turn of phrase."

Drew kept one ear on the conversation as he turned to assist the ladies with their wraps. Lady Charlotte had already shed her heavy ermine-lined cloak and was walking toward the stairs, while Lady Melanie stood quietly, not seeming to notice the footman who stood waiting to help her out of her velvet cape. For a moment Drew thought that perhaps she was waiting for him to help her, then he saw her face.

"Is there anything amiss, my lady?" Drew stepped forward impulsively, his one thought to comfort her. She looked so lost and alone, and for a brief moment he had seen a look of blank terror mirrored in the purple depths of her eyes.

Melanie stirred at Davies's words, blinking her eyes at the urgency of his tone. "Not at all, Davies," she told him, mentally marshaling her forces. Her lips quivered as she attempted a weak smile. "Is Miss Evingale still awake, or is she long abed?"

"I believe she has retired, my lady," Drew answered, aware that she was avoiding his question. His eyes narrowed slightly, and for a brief moment he resented the necessity of his deception. Had he been able to appear before her as an equal, as a gentleman, he would have insisted she answer him.

"Well, then perhaps I shall as well," Melanie answered with forced brightness, turning to kiss her father's cheek. "Good night, Papa, sleep well."

"You, too, my dear," he answered affectionately, giving her hand a fond pat. "And mind that you sleep until noon, as befits a proper lady, hmm? Perhaps that will put the roses back in your cheeks."

"If you say so, sir." She smiled up at him once more, then turned to Mr. Barrymore, holding her hand out to him and realizing much to her chagrin that she had ignored him ever since she had overheard that conversation. She couldn't even remember if she had given him the dance she had promised him.

"Good night, Mr. Barrymore," she said, offering him a cautious smile. "I hope I shall see you in the morning."

"Thank you, my lady." He bowed graciously over her hand, his blue eyes sharp as they studied her. "And thank you also for our dance. I enjoyed it excessively."

"You're welcome, sir." She was relieved that she hadn't been so distracted that she had broken her

78

word. "And I am glad that you enjoyed your evening."

His smile widened a fraction. "You may rest assured, my lady, I found the experience to be most edifying. Most edifying indeed."

It was four o'clock. Melanie lay quietly in her bed listening to the ancient clock in the hallway tolling out the hour. She had been awake for the past two hours, thoughts racing through her head. Her one impulse was to protect her father at all cost, but she knew it would be better if she told him everything, including the unpleasant scene with Mrs. Mason, she thought, finally understanding what lay behind the other woman's animosity.

It also explained why her father had been relegated to so trifling a position when logic dictated a man with his experience should have been placed elsewhere. If the Foreign Secretary felt her father was disloyal, then she knew the evidence against him had to be damning. Despite what others might think of Lord Castlereagh, Melanie knew him to be scrupulously honest, and she knew he would never condemn a man without sufficient cause.

She turned on her back, staring up at the ceiling with eyes that burned with weariness. She would give much to learn what evidence had been gathered against her father, and even more to learn who had gathered it. Her papa had no enemies of whom she was aware, and yet it was obvious that someone had deliberately set out to ruin him. She couldn't imagine anyone going to such lengths to implicate an innocent man unless—she frowned suddenly— unless *they* were the guilty party!

That was it, she thought, sitting up in the bed, her bedcovers tumbling to her waist. Some villain was betraying England and using her father to cover his crimes! Just like that awful Count whatever-his-name in one of the books Miss Evingale had read to her. He pretended to be the heroine's loving guardian, when all along he was scheming to deprive her of her fortune and her life. Count Cruello, that was the wretch's name, and he—she pulled herself up short as she realized the direction of her thoughts.

Lord, she had to be half crazed to give those silly books a moment's credence. The danger facing her father was all too real, and she could never hope to save him if she gave way to silly fancies. If she wanted to defeat her enemy, then she would have to be just as clever and just as ruthless as he was. Melanie was no fool; she knew what she was planning was both dangerous and daring, but she had no other choice. To save her father she would have to catch the real spy herself.

Chapter Six

Despite an almost sleepless night, Melanie rose early the next morning, determined to confront her father. She knew he usually left for Whitehall after breakfast, and she rushed downstairs to join him. Both he and Mr. Barrymore were already seated, and they glanced up at her arrival.

"Why, Melanie, whatever are you doing up at this hour?" the earl asked, his eyebrows climbing in surprise. "After last night I was certain you would sleep till noon."

"I—I was wondering if I might have a word with you, Papa," she stammered, clasping her hands together to hide their nervous trembling.

"Of course, my dear, of course." Lord Terrington smiled at her quizzically. "But won't you eat something first? I'm certain you must be famished. Davies"—he turned to the ever-present butler—"have the footman fetch my daughter a—"

"No!" Melanie interrupted, her eyes flicking first to Mr. Barrymore, who was regarding her with polite inquiry, to Davies, who stood expressionless at her father's side. "That is, I'm not very hungry," she added somewhat lamely, "and I really would like to speak with you . . . alone."

"Ah, it must be serious, then," the earl laughed, exchanging a knowing smile with his assistant. "I thought your last modiste's bill was rather modest, now I can see I may have been a trifle premature. Very well, Melanie." He set his napkin down and rose to his feet. "I suppose I shall let you talk your poor father into buying you another gown or two."

Melanie remained silent as they walked to his study, wishing that a new wardrobe were the only thing she had to discuss with him. Poor Papa, he was going to be so shocked when she told him her news, so hurt.

"Now, there's no need to look so pensive, my dear," Lord Terrington said as he settled behind his mahogany desk. "I was only funning you. Naturally, you may have as many gowns as you wish."

"Thank you, Papa, but that isn't why I asked to speak with you," she began, realizing this was proving much harder than she had anticipated. She sat in her chair, winding the cherry silk ribbon of her gown around her finger as she struggled for the words to tell him.

"Papa, there is talk you are a traitor," she blurted out, unable to meet his gaze. "They are saying you have sold us out to the French."

"I know."

The softly spoken admission brought her head snapping up. "You—you know?" she whispered in disbelief.

"For some time now," he confessed, his gentle gray eyes meeting hers. "But I had hoped that you would be spared from the rumors. I am sorry, child."

"But how can they say such dreadful things about you?" she cried, leaning forward to study his grim face. "What proof have they to even suggest such a thing?"

"Several of my dispatches disappeared during our last year in Washington," he explained with a heavy sigh, thrusting a hand through his thinning gray hair. "Nothing specific has ever been said, mind you, but I would be a fool not to know that the government suspects me. Tell me what you have heard."

Melanie dutifully related the conversation she had overheard, as well as the details of her encounter with Mrs. Mason. As she suspected, her father was outraged.

"Why, that disagreeable old crow, how dare she treat you so!" he exclaimed, his eyes flashing with anger. "If her husband weren't such a capable administrator, I vow I would have him posted in the worst hole I could find!" He stopped abruptly, his lips twisting in an ironic smile. "Provided, of course, that I haven't been sent there yet myself. I fear your papa is sailing in rather deep waters, Melanie, my love."

Melanie's heart constricted at his words. Her hands sought his both to give comfort and take comfort. "Will you be arrested?" she asked, remembering the unknown woman's vicious remarks about his probable fate.

"I don't know," the earl confessed softly, "as I have said, there have been no direct accusations, just certain looks, whispered comments that one can never quite catch, and, of course, there was my rather hasty recall from America. I know I am suspected, but there is little I can do about it."

"You can fight!" Melanie cried, blinking back tears of anger. "Make them tell you what it is they think you've done, and then make them prove it! You're a good man, Papa, you don't deserve to be treated like this!"

"Ah, my little warrior, if only it were that simple." Lord Terrington brushed a loving finger across Melanie's flushed cheek. "Don't you think I haven't thought the very same thing? But one cannot fight a ghost, Melanie. Until I know who my accuser is, it is safest to wait."

"But Papa—"

There was a knock at the door, and Mr. Barrymore looked in, a hesitant smile hovering on his lips. "Forgive the intrusion, my lord," he said diffidently. "But we ought to be leaving if we hope to meet with Lord Raynard before the debating session begins."

"Very well, Mr. Barrymore, thank you. I shall be with you in a moment," the earl said politely, his stern glance silencing the protest forming on Melanie's lips. "And be so good as to close the door behind you, won't you?"

"Papa, you can't go now!" she exclaimed once they were alone again. "We must plot our strategy and decide what we are to do!"

"I have already told you what I intend doing," her father said in his most authoritative manner. "Nothing. And I am ordering you to do the same."

"But you cannot mean you mean to sit here meekly until they cart you off to Newgate!" she cried, leaping angrily to her feet. "What about the real villain; have you thought of him?"

"What villain? Really, Melanie, I fear you have

been listening to Miss Evingale again." The earl shook his head at her. "There is no villain, real or otherwise. It is all a dreadful misunderstanding, and one that will be cleared up if you stay out of it." He rose belatedly to his feet, bending his head to press a kiss to her cheek.

"I know you mean well, dearest," he said, gazing down into her turbulent eyes with fatherly affection, "but I must insist that you forget all this foolish nonsense and let me do the worrying, hmm? It will all turn out well in the end, you'll see."

After he had departed, Melanie went storming up to her rooms, venting her frustrations by slamming the door as hard as she could. How could any man as intelligent as her papa be so foolishly blind to the truth, she fumed, pacing the room in her agitation. Why did he refuse to admit the danger when it was dangling over his very head? And that mocking comment of his that she had been listening to Miss Evingale again . . . she could cheerfully have throttled him for that. Couldn't he see she was only trying to help?

Well, he could close his eyes and play the blindman if he chose, Melanie decided abruptly. But she had no intention of sitting quietly by while her father was arrested and hung for a crime he had not committed. The villain she had tried to warn him of was as real as any creature out of Miss Evingale's Minervian novels, and she would catch him any way she could. And with that thought she turned and walked out of her room, her expression determined as she knocked on her companion's door.

". . . and *Lady Devore's Masquerade*, that one had the most wonderfully gruesome ghost; I couldn't sleep a wink for days!" Miss Evingale concluded, adding another book to the growing pile in Melanie's arms. "That should be more than enough to get you started; you must come back for more when you are finished with them."

"I'm sure this will be more than adequate, thank you," Melanie replied, fumbling for the doorknob with her free hand. Her companion was regarding her with the zealous fervor of a missionary with a new convert, and she was eager to escape before another volume was pressed upon her.

"Well, if you're sure that will be enough." Miss Evingale was eyeing her dubiously. "They make for very quick reading, you know, and you can't have more than a dozen or so. Perhaps one more . . ."

"No, really, this is more than enough, I promise you." Melanie opened the door and began inching her way out. "I'll give these to Grandmother when I have—"

"The Castle of Montenegro," Miss Evingale interrupted, pulling a leather-bound volume from beneath the tea table and waving it at Melanie in triumph. "It's one of my favorites, and I'm sure you will adore it. The villain is a curate who tries to entomb the heroine when she discovers his dreadful secret. You did say you wanted something with a dash of mystery, didn't you?"

"Indeed, I did," Melanie agreed, accepting the book with a resigned sigh. "Thank you."

"Do you know, I am rather surprised that you should want to borrow my novels," Miss Evingale said abruptly, her brows puckering in a confused frown. "I had formed the opinion that you weren't overly fond of them."

"Well, it is true that I am not quite the devotee

as you and Grandmother," Melanie agreed mendaciously, mentally crossing her fingers. "But I have decided that perhaps a bit of romance and mystery in one's life is not so terrible a thing after all. Good day, Edwina, I shall see you at luncheon."

Once safely in her rooms, Melanie dismissed her maid and spread the books out on her bed. The titles were really quite appalling, she mused, picking up a book and flicking it open to read the contents. But perhaps if she was lucky, she might find something that would prove helpful. Ah, she paused, her lips lifting in a pleased smile as she read a passage. This looked promising.

In the most hidden recesses of her heart Lady Cassiopia knew she had no other choice. Her murdered brother's spirit called out to her from the nether world, demanding revenge upon the archvillain who had taken his life. To ignore his ghostly cry was impossible, and so she bravely set aside her own tremulous fear and reached out for the doorknob to Roberto's secret chamber.

By the time the maid returned to help her dress for dinner that night, Melanie had already finished the first book and was well into the second. Miss Evingale was right, she thought as the maid arranged her hair in a lover's knot. The books did make for fast reading, which was probably fortunate, as they were so badly written. But the flowery prose and cloying sentimentality aside, she had discovered that the books all seemed to share a common theme: Nothing was ever as it first appeared.

The lowliest of scullery maids would prove to be a long-lost princess, highborn lords or ladies were inevitably scheming servants who had usurped their master's position, and the closest of friends was revealed in the final pages of the story to be the most deadly of enemies. It was this last revelation that troubled her most, for it seemed to verify her suspicion that whoever was betraying Papa was someone they both knew and trusted.

They were to dine at the home of Lord Canaby, a former diplomat once stationed in New York, so Melanie was not surprised to learn that Mr. Barrymore was to join them. It did surprise her, however, when he asked to speak with her privately while they were waiting for the carriage to be brought around.

"Certainly, Mr. Barrymore," she answered, shooting him a quizzical look. "Is there something amiss?"

"Not at all," he assured her, guiding her into the earl's study. "But I thought we should talk. You see, your father has told me that you have learned of the vicious rumors that are being circulated about him."

"Do you mean *you* knew, too?" Melanie asked, feeling faintly shocked by the admission. Good heavens, was she the only one in London who didn't know, she wondered unhappily.

"I am your father's assistant," Mr. Barrymore answered, sitting behind the earl's desk. "It is only natural to assume that if he is under suspicion, then so am I. That is what I wished to speak to you about."

"What do you mean?" Melanie asked, the plot of the book she was now reading springing unbidden to her mind. Although she was only halfway through the story, she strongly suspected the villain would turn out to be the earnest young man who was always warning the heroine away from the locked cellar door.

"Your father said that you were quite upset by what you heard, and that you thought he should take some sort of action. Is that not so?"

"Yes," she agreed cautiously, studying him through half-lowered lashes.

"As it happens, I agree with you," Mr. Barrymore said, his blue eyes twinkling at her look of astonishment. "I take it you thought I would share his sentiments?"

Melanie nodded, her shoulders slumping with relief as she realized she now had an ally. "I admit the possibility did cross my mind," she admitted, giving him a cautious smile. "Papa was so adamant that nothing be done that I feared you might feel the same. I cannot tell you how pleased I am to learn that such is not the case."

"Not at all," he assured her, his expression serious. "In fact, I even agree with your charge that your father is being set to take the blame for another's crime. Do you have any idea who the villain might be? Other than myself, that is."

"You?" She stared at him in shock.

He shrugged his shoulders. "It's a logical assumption, my lady," he said simply. "As his assistant, I have access to the missing documents, and, of course, I am not of noble birth."

"Mr. Barrymore!" Her cheeks pinked with embarrassed color as she realized she had suspected him. "I am sure such a notion never crossed my mind! And the matter of your birth is of little consequence to me, I assure you."

"Your ladyship is too kind, but there are others of your class who are not quite so generous," Mr. Barrymore said, a trace of bitterness evident in his soft voice. "If your father has been the object of a few questioning glances of late, it is nothing compared to what *I* have endured! There are several men in power who would as lief see me hang as to let one of their own stand accused of treason. That is why I must ask your help."

"What is it you need?"

"I want you to keep your ears open," he instructed Melanie gently, leaning forward to meet her gaze. "Go to as many balls as you can, and listen for any word, any hint, that might lead us to the real traitor. The moment you hear anything, I want you to come directly to me."

"Is that all?" Melanie felt vaguely disappointed; even the foolish, swooning heroine in this newest book had more to do than just that.

"It's more than enough, I promise you." Mr. Barrymore's voice was grim. "You see, as an outsider I am not privy to the types of conversation you will be hearing. And I think we both agree that our villain is of the nobility?"

"Well, yes, I suppose so," Melanie agreed reluctantly. "Certainly he is someone Papa must know and trust. How else would he have had access to his dispatch box?"

"My sentiments exactly. And because he is probably one of your own class, you stand the best chance to help trap him. No one would ever suspect you of trying to trap him, would they?"

This was true, Melanie was forced to agree, and put that way, it did sound rather intriguing. She could pretend to be enjoying herself at every rout and ball in London, and all the while she would be helping Papa to clear his name! Yes, the more she thought of it, the more she decided it was just the sort of thing the heroine in one of her books might do.

"Very well, Mr. Barrymore," she said, her violet eyes taking on an excited glow. "I shall do as you ask. I shall keep my eyes and ears open, and the moment I hear anything of importance, I shall come to you at once."

"Excellent!" He gave her a brilliant smile. "And while you're busy doing that, I shall be attempting to determine the source of these rumors. We know they started in Whitehall, but that is all we have been able to learn. With any luck, we shall discover the blackguard's true identity before your father's reputation is irreparably damaged. Now, come." He rose to his feet, offering her his hand. "It is time I returned you to your father, else it is *your* reputation that is damaged."

"Damn it all. Now what the devil are we going to do?" Drew muttered angrily, his hazel eyes flashing with fire as he watched the carriage drive away.

When Mr. Barrymore had taken Lady Melanie into the earl's study, he had followed them, slipping into the room off the hall, where he could listen to their conversation undetected. He told himself it was necessary that he do so, but he knew it was really because he found the notion of Melanie going off for a private conversation with Barrymore oddly disturbing. Certainly he hadn't seen fit to do so when she had spoken with her father earlier this morning, a rather unfortunate oversight on his part, it would seem. Terrington knew everything!

Another thing which troubled him was the rumor that was already being circulated about the earl.

Secrecy was vital to a successful mission, and if Terrington was aware he was under suspicion, then he would be that much more difficult to catch. And if he was not guilty, then the same could be said about the real culprit. Quarry that knew the hunter was there invariably escaped the trap.

His frown deepened as he thought of what Barrymore had said to Melanie. Logically he would have been suspected first when the documents were discovered missing, and for the very reason he gave her. His birth would have automatically made him suspect in the rather insular world of diplomatic circles, yet a very high-ranking official in that group had vouchsafed his character above one of his own. Why? That was the one piece of the puzzle he had yet to learn.

"Beggin' your pardon, Mr. Davies." Grisby, Barrymore's valet, appeared at Drew's side, a hopeful expression on his weasellike face. "But I was wonderin' if I might be havin' the rest of the night off? Mr. Barrymore usually gives me the third Thursday free, so's I can go see me sister."

"Then as it is the third Thursday, Grisby, I suppose I have no objection," Drew replied, slipping easily into his role of an upperservant lording it over one he considered an inferior. "Will you be gone all night?"

"Oh, can't be sayin', Mr. Davies," Grisby said, giving him a broad wink. "Depends on me sister, if ye takes my meaning. But I reckons ye'll see me when ye see me."

"We will be locking the doors one hour after his lordship and his party return home, Grisby." As a butler, Drew did not lower himself to gossip with the valet. "If you aren't in your room, then I fear you will have to seek accommodations elsewhere.

Also, will Mr. Barrymore be requiring the services of one of our footmen in your stead?"

"Nah, his nibs can do just fine on his own." Grisby dismissed his employer with a cavalier shrug of his beefy shoulders. " 'Sides, Mr. Barrymore be almighty particular about his fancy clothes an' them sparklers o' his. Don't let nobody but ol' Grisby touch 'em," he added, his chest swelling with pride.

Drew was careful to hide his interest. Until now Grisby had been tight-lipped to the point of being suspiciously secretive, but apparently the thought of a few hours pleasure in his doxy's arms had loosened his tongue, and Drew was eager to exploit the fact. Calling upon a servant's usual tendency to brag about his employer, he allowed a faintly skeptical expression to flit across his face.

"Indeed?" he asked coolly. "I have yet to see Mr. Barrymore wearing any sort of jewelry. However, there is a fine safe in the house should he wish to keep his watch fobs there."

"Watch fobs?" Grisby's cheeks puffed out with indignation. "Mr. Barrymore has a lot more'n watch fobs! Why, that last sparkler o' his were as big as me thumb! An' plen'y more where that come from, he tole me!"

"I see." Drew resolved to search Barrymore's rooms the moment Grisby left. "Well, then I should definitely suggest to Mr. Barrymore that he avail himself of our safe. His Grace has an excellent one hidden in his private chambers."

"Mr. Barrymore don't need your tin safe!" Grisby sniffed with disdain. "He can take care of what's his, don' you be worryin'. He carries a brace o'pistols with him, an' he'll use 'em, too, if anyone was to come snoopin' around. He's bang up to the nines, is my Mr. Barrymore!"

"The duke has an armory at his estate in the country." Drew defended his alleged employer with the dogged loyalty of an old retainer. "And he is both a skilled marksman and a fencer of some note."

They spent another few minutes extolling the virtues of their respective employers, and when Drew felt he had soothed any suspicions Grisby might be harboring, he said, "You may go now, if you wish, Grisby. As I said, we lock the doors one hour after the earl's return. If you aren't in, then you will have to spend the night in the cold."

"Oh, I won't be cold, guv'." Grisby forgot himself enough to poke Drew in the ribs, a lascivious grin spreading across his face. "See you on the morrow, then."

Less than twenty minutes later Drew was staring down at a large diamond fob, a soundless whistle pursing his lips. Whatever his other faults, it was obvious Grisby wasn't prone to exaggeration. The diamond in his hand was at least two carats in weight, and the chain it was hanging from was pure gold. He turned it over, noting the small crest that had been stamped into the shiny metal. He held it closer to the flickering candlelight, his brows meeting in a frown as he studied the design. There was something about it that was vaguely familiar; then he remembered the ruby ring.

Two minutes later he held the ring and fob side by side, studying the feathered crest carefully. It was a heraldic device, that much he could tell, but it wasn't one he recognized. He took a piece of paper and pen from the desk and traced the crest to show Sir, reasoning that if anyone would know what it meant, it would be his superior.

That done, he conducted a quick search of Barrymore's private correspondence, looking for anything that might explain his sudden affluence. He found several bills from his tailor, all marked paid, and a few markers for gaming debts, but nothing of a more personal nature. Disgusted, he was about to give up when something made him take a closer look at the name on one of the markers. Parkinson. He stared at the name, wondering why he should recognize it, then in a flash it came to him. Parkinson was Lord Marlehope's son and heir, and, if memory served, an up-and-coming officer in the Foreign Service.

Using the same pen and paper he had used to copy the crest, Drew transcribed the marker for Sir. He was certain Sir would be interested in the connection, especially if it had been Marlehope who had arranged for Barrymore to be hired by Terrington; and Marlehope who swore to Barrymore's innocence in the matter now under investigation. All in all a good night's work, he decided, giving the room a final glance to make sure he had left no trace of his snooping behind. Sir would be pleased.

Melanie spent the next week attending every ball to which she had been invited and studiously devouring the Gothics Miss Evingale had lent her. Although she learned little of interest with her eavesdropping, she did find the novels to be most instructive, and she soon grew restive to act upon her newfound knowledge. The first thing she decided she must do was to take a more active role in the mystery.

In her Gothics the heroines were forever sneaking about, peeking into locked drawers and snooping around abandoned dungeons. There were no dungeons in Marchfield House, but there was a locked drawer in the desk in Papa's study. If she was to clear his name, she decided, she would have to know what was inside.

She waited until Papa and Mr. Barrymore had left for the day before making her try. It was the day before her presentation, and with the household so distracted, she was certain no one would notice her stealing into her father's study. Not that it should really matter, she thought, creeping down the hallway. It was Papa's house, after all, and if anyone should dare question her, she could simply say she was looking for something. But in the books, stealth was indicated as being of major importance, and she thought it best not to quibble with the experts.

The room looked perfectly ordinary in the bright sunlight pouring through the open drapes, and for a moment Melanie was vaguely disappointed. It would have been much more intriguing if she'd had to do her snooping in a dark and deserted monastery, as had Constance Bartholomew in *The Sinister Hand*. She crossed the pale cream and blue carpet to the desk, extracting the butter knife she had slipped into her pocket a few minutes earlier. In another moment she was behind the desk, regarding the shiny brass lock with a frown. The author had simply written that Constance had used a knife to open the rusty lock on the poor box, but she hadn't indicated precisely how this was accomplished. Ah, well. She shrugged her slender shoulders and bent her head over the desk, cautiously prying at the drawer with the flat edge of the knife.

From his position behind the drapes, Drew

watched her amateurish probings with grim interest. He had seen her stealthy progress down the hall, and realizing she was heading for the study, he had quickly availed himself of the secret passage into the room which Marchfield had prudently shown him. He had barely hidden himself behind the drapes when she slipped soundlessly into the room.

So Melanie was involved, he thought angrily, his hands clenching into tight fists. The little baggage! And here he had all but convinced Sir that the real traitor was Barrymore. Not that he could entirely rule the assistant out, of course. The two could well be working as confederates. But why? What possible reason could Melanie have for putting her head in a noose? The only reason he could think of was love, and he was shocked to discover that he found the thought of Melanie in love with Barrymore almost as hateful as the notion of her being involved in treason.

The sound of wood giving way was followed by Melanie's soft gasp of delight as the knife fell to the floor. He ventured a cautious peek around the edge of the crimson velvet drape, watching as she lifted the sealed papers from the drawer.

"It worked!" she exclaimed triumphantly, lifting the first document and peeking at its contents eagerly. She found nothing of interest and set it down, studying the remaining papers with the same hopeful caution. It was only as she examined all of them that she realized that she had no notion of what she should be searching for. Papa had said only that some of his dispatches had found their way into enemy hands, but he had never told her precisely what those dispatches contained. Nor would he, she realized glumly. Papa never discussed such things with her.

Glancing down at the papers in her hand, a faint sense of shame and embarrassment began creeping over her. She had broken into the duke's desk and betrayed her father's trust in her, and all for naught. Clearly she was not destined to be a heroine, she decided with a heavy sigh as she rose to her feet.

She was returning the papers to the desk when the sensation she was being watched stole over her. She'd felt tendrils of the sensation earlier when she had forced the lock, but she had shrugged the feeling aside as guilt. Now there was no ignoring the sickening feeling of awareness that was hammering at her consciousness. Taking a deep breath to steady her racing pulses, she whirled around to confront her unseen observer. There was nothing, not even the slightest movement or sound to indicate another's presence in the study.

Melanie eyed the drapes cautiously, even taking a step toward them before she realized how foolishly she was behaving. Idiot! She gave a self-conscious laugh, mentally scolding herself for acting in such a missish fashion. Of course there was no one in the room. The only way into the room was through the door, and she would have known if anyone had entered. Shaking her head at her own gullibility, she straightened her skirts and quietly exited the room.

It was only when she was halfway up the stairs that she remembered the butter knife lying on the carpet. If it were discovered, then someone would know Papa's desk had been searched, and she shuddered to think of the havoc it would wreak were she found to be the culprit. Repressing a small sigh, she turned and retraced her steps to the study.

She would also have to think of some way of returning the knife to the kitchens, Melanie realized, opening the door and walking over to the desk. Apparently there was more to this investigating business than she had first supposed, she mused, her lips quirking in a smile as she bent down to retrieve the knife. It was gone.

Chapter Seven

Melanie stared at the blank expanse of carpet in stunned dismay. It had to be here, she thought frantically, scrambling around on her knees as her fingers felt under the desk. There was nothing, no sign of the knife or the mysterious forces that had spirited it away. She sat back on her haunches, forcing her frozen mind to function.

Perhaps one of the servants had innocently happened along, and finding the knife, had simply returned it to the kitchens. But even as this thought occurred to her, she rejected it. She had been gone from the room less than a minute, and there was no way a servant, or anyone else for that matter, could have slipped out of the room and down the hall without her seeing them, which left only one logical conclusion, she realized, her stomach clenching with dread. Someone *had* been in the room with her.

But who, and why had he taken her knife with him? Both Mr. Barrymore and her father had been gone for well over an hour, and she found it difficult to envision either Miss Evingale or her grandmother behaving in so clandestine a fashion. Her companion lacked the wit to carry the thing off successfully, and such subtlety was beyond Lady Charlotte's abrasive but forthright personality. Which left the servants, she decided, her eyes narrowing in suspicion. And she thought she might have a very good idea what servant that might be. Davies.

She thought of everything she did and did not know of him. He was young, much too young to be a butler, and far too handsome as well. In the past week she had been in any number of elegant London homes, and not a single butler she had seen looked anything like Davies. Then there was the time she had caught him in the study, standing beside this very desk. And he knew what a hakim was, she remembered, struggling awkwardly to her feet. If he was not the villain, she would eat each and every one of Miss Evingale's Gothics!

But in the next moment she was frowning again. It couldn't be Davies, she realized, her confusion mounting. Papa said the dispatches had disappeared during their last year in Washington, and Davies had been safely tucked away on the Duke of Marchfield's country estates at that time. Or had he? She shook her head in bewilderment. None of this made the slightest bit of sense to her.

On the one hand, Davies was the only possible suspect, but on the other hand, he couldn't possibly be involved in whatever mischief was afoot. But whatever the case, she vowed she would keep a closer eye on the butler. If he made any movement she considered suspicious, then she would decide what she must do.

* * *

After returning the knife to the pantry, Drew retired to his room to pace and think. Now, here was a fine kettle of fish, and no mistake about it, he thought, raking an impatient hand through his tousled hair. What had Melanie been thinking when she came creeping into that study? She hadn't even opened some of those documents, and the others she had discarded after scarcely glancing at them. If she'd been looking for something important, wouldn't she have taken greater care in examining the papers? And if she wasn't looking for anything specific, then why had she broken into the desk in the first place? He shook his head. This was without doubt the most convoluted mission he had ever undertaken for Sir, and he wished to heaven it was over.

He paused in his pacing to study his reflection in the mirror; the frown wrinkling his brow growing more pronounced as he remembered Melanie's conversation with Barrymore. She had been so eloquent in her father's defense, and so patently eager to help prove his innocence. Why then would she turn around and search his office without his permission? Unless—his golden-brown eyebrows met over the bridge of his nose—unless she had broken into the desk looking for some sort of information that would help her clear his name.

No, he dismissed the thought angrily, not even Melanie could be that big of a gudgeon. And yet, he admitted with mounting exasperation, it sounded precisely like something the minx would do. She was as obstinate and headstrong as she was beautiful, and he could easily imagine her devising such a stratagem.

The realization that he was allowing his partiality for Melanie to delude him occurred to Drew, and he was too good an agent to ignore the possibility. With so much at stake, he knew he dared not trust his own judgment in the matter, and he decided he would have to confide in Sir.

The Terringtons would be dining out this evening, which meant he would have at least four hours to himself. He could slip over to Sir's rooms near Covent Garden for a quick conference and be back in Mayfair long before the family returned home. Drew's eyes flicked to the small clock on his bedside table. It was almost noon; with any luck Sir would still be at home. He'd send a message requesting a meeting, and hopefully he would receive a reply by the time the family had left. If not, he'd simply have to risk contacting Sir on his own. Events were moving rather quickly now, and his excellently honed senses warned him they were approaching a crisis point. And when that point came, Drew was determined to be ready for any eventuality.

"You aren't accompanying the others tonight?" Drew asked, staring at Melanie in dismay. "Is there some sort of problem, my lady?"

"Not at all, Davies," Melanie replied serenely, her expression cool as she studied the butler's unhappy countenance. "I simply didn't feel like dining out this evening. Why?" She turned the tables on him with a sweet smile.

"No reason, Lady Melanie," Drew said, masking his anger at her sardonic reply. He might have known the little she-devil would manage to throw a spanner into his carefully laid plans, he thought, his agile mind working to overcome this newest difficulty. "I was merely concerned that you might not be feeling well, that is all."

"Oh, I am in the best of health," she assured him with a glittering smile. "But as tomorrow night is my presentation at Court, I thought it best to make an early night of it. I shall be retiring quite shortly, as a matter of fact."

"A wise plan, my lady," Drew agreed with relief. With her tucked snugly in her bed there was still a chance he could slip away from the house undetected.

"I am glad you approve," Melanie murmured, trying not to laugh at the scheming look that stole across Davies's face. She could swear she could hear the thoughts racing inside his head, and what she heard reaffirmed her decision to remain at home rather than spend another useless evening listening to the same old tired gossip.

She had gotten the idea from one of Miss Evingale's newer books, *The Dreadful House of Clymsford*, wherein the clever heroine pretended to be asleep while the villain was skulking about doing his evil deeds. That Flavia was entombed in a crypt for her pains was dismissed as unimportant, for she had eventually found her way out. What mattered most was that the villain had been lulled into a false sense of security by the heroine's actions, thereby bringing about his own downfall. She had no idea what Davies might be up to, but she was resolved to find out.

"Would you care for a glass of milk before you retire, my lady?" Drew asked solicitously, remembering the laudanum Mrs. Musgrove kept locked in her cupboard for the maids. "It might be just the thing to help you sleep."

Melanie was sure it would, being liberally laced

with heaven only knew what kind of heathenish potion. "That sounds lovely, Davies, thank you, although I'm sure it won't be necessary," she answered, stifling a delicate yawn behind her hand. "I am so fagged, I vow I shall sleep until morning. Please see to it that I'm not disturbed, won't you?"

"Very good, my lady, and I will have one of the maids bring you the milk in the event you should want it," Drew said, pleased with the way things had worked out. With Melanie lightly drugged with laudanum, he would have no difficulty keeping his rendezvous with Sir. "Sleep well."

"Oh, I will," Melanie demurred, praying she hadn't overplayed her hand, possibly alerting him to her true purpose. "Good night, Davies."

Once in her room, she had the maid assist her into her nightrail, yawning and rubbing at her eyes like an exhausted child. As she expected, a second maid appeared with an appetizing glass of warm milk, dusted with enough nutmeg to mask whatever drug may have been added. She pretended to drink it, but the moment the maid's back was turned she dumped the suspicious mixture into the chamber pot. Satisfied she had succeeded in duping the young girl, she climbed into bed, sleepily bidding her a good night as the door closed.

Melanie spent the next half hour waiting in the darkness until she was certain the maid wouldn't return, then she got up and cautiously lit one candle, hurriedly donning her oldest gown of blue serge. This accomplished, she extinguished the candle and got back into bed, pulling the covers up over her head. She hadn't long to wait; scarce twenty minutes later the door creaked open, and two figures stealthily approached the bed.

"There you see, Mr. Davies," the young maid who

had assisted her whispered eagerly, " 'tis just as I said, the poor wee thing was that tired. She barely stayed awake long enough for me to tuck her into bed."

"Are you certain she drank the milk?" Drew asked softly, bending over Melanie and watching the even rise and fall of her breasts beneath the rose counterpane. Her cheeks were warm and slightly flushed, and in the faint light from the hallway he could see the shadows cast by her thick lashes. A strand of black hair lay across her high cheekbone, and it took every ounce of will he possessed not to brush it aside.

"Every drop, sir," he was assured by the breathless maid. "My lady even complained there was too much nutmeg, and asked me to tell Mrs. Musgrove."

He smiled at that. "I shall tell her myself," he said, turning away from the bed. "In the meanwhile, I want you to check on her every half hour. She should sleep well until morning, but in the event she wakens, try to keep her in the room. I don't know what time I will be returning, and I don't want to find her roaming the halls when I do."

"Very good, Mr. Davies," the maid agreed, trailing him to the door. "I'll tell Millie, too, mayhap she will help me keep watch." And the door closed behind them.

Melanie waited for another ten minutes, then scrambled hurriedly from the bed. Not daring to risk lighting another candle, she found her shoes in the darkness, slipping her bare feet into the soft leather slippers. She fumbled for her cape, flinging it about her shoulders and then racing from the room as silently as a ghost.

There was no one about as she crept down the stairs, although she could hear the sound of laughter coming from the servants' hall. Well, let them laugh, she decided crossly, her fingers shaking as she cautiously lifted the door latch. It would seem the entire household, including the motherly Mrs. Musgrove, was involved in Davies's nefarious plot, and the very notion filled her with indignation. Was there no one she could trust, she wondered somewhat angrily.

It was cool outside, the late April evening still carrying a touch of winter's chill. Melanie's slippered feet made no noise as she crossed the cobblestoned street, hiding herself behind a neighbor's house, where she could watch the back of her own house without being seen. She waited for what seemed an eternity before a caped figure came out the servants' exit. She had no trouble recognizing Davies's broad shoulders and proud carriage as he turned down the street, his long-legged stride making it difficult for her to keep up with him.

Drew kept his head down, his collar turned up against the damp wind as he walked purposefully toward the inn where he had arranged to meet Sir. There was much he had to tell his superior, and he found himself dreading what his reaction might be. Although he admired Sir and would willingly lay down his life on his behalf, there was no denying that the man was as cold and ruthless as the sea. If he believed Melanie to be involved in whatever rig Barrymore was running, then he would be totally without mercy.

A carriage rumbling by made Drew pause at the corner, and as was his habit, he stole a quick glance over his shoulder. The small figure emerging out of the ever-deepening fog made him tense, his hand reaching automatically for the knife in his pocket. But as the figure drew closer, he could see it was only a housemaid doubtlessly scurrying to an assignation of her own, and he turned away in disinterest.

The streets around the small tavern where he was to meet Sir were filled with revelers, and more than once Drew had to step aside to let them pass. He had almost reached The Blue Stallion when he heard a sharp cry behind him. He turned around in time to see the small maid, who was apparently still following him, being dragged into the darkened alleyway by a burly-set man. Cursing the man's poor sense of timing, he pulled the knife from his pocket and raced into the alley after them.

Melanie never even saw the man. One moment Davies was just ahead of her, and the next a strong set of arms had closed about her, a hard and filthy hand clamping over her mouth and choking off her scream. Despite her terror, Melanie fought with all her strength, her heavy skirts hampering her attempts to free herself. Her struggles only seemed to amuse her captor, who flung her against the brick wall in back of her, his brutal hands tearing at her cloak.

"Come on, dearie, give us a peek, eh?" He laughed drunkenly, his slurred words increasing Melanie's terror as it dawned on her what he intended to do. "Ol' Ben just wants some lovin', there's my girl." He slipped a hand inside her cloak, grabbing at the tender flesh beneath.

"No!" Melanie screamed, struggling furiously to free herself from this nightmarish situation. "Let me go!"

"Hush, you bitch!" Her assailant clamped his hand back over her mouth and nose, shutting off her air and making it impossible to breathe. Melanie fought against the darkness that swirled around her, sheer terror giving her a strength she did not know she possessed.

Just as she was certain she would surely faint, the man holding her gave a convulsive jerk, his eyes widening for a moment and then slowly going blank as he slumped against her, his body sliding to the filthy stones.

Melanie first thought he must have passed out from drink, then in the flickering light of the torch burning near the alleyway's entrance, she saw the handle of the blade protruding from his back. She swayed on her feet, her mouth opening for the scream that was caught in her throat. Bright lights danced before her eyes as she tried to force her voice to work.

"Are you all right?" Another pair of arms, just as strong as the first man's but strangely different, slipped around Melanie's waist, guiding her gently from the alley. "Don't worry about that vermin, he won't cause you any further trouble. Poor child, did he hurt you?"

The voice was tender and reassuring and oddly familiar as well. Slowly Melanie managed to raise her head, violet eyes made wide from shock resting on her rescuer's face. "Davies," she said quite clearly, and then fainted into Drew's waiting arms.

"I didn't know what else to do," a frantic voice emerged out of the safe gray fog that sheltered Melanie, disturbing her slumber and making her faintly fretful, and she willed it to go away. "She'd fainted dead away from the shock."

"I agree you could hardly leave her lying on the

sidewalk, but you must realize this does complicate matters. I suppose I needn't ask what happened to the whoreson that attacked her?" A second voice was speaking, and Melanie's brows puckered faintly. What were all these men doing in her bed-chamber? It didn't seem quite proper to her.

"Dead. I left my best knife in his back, too, blast it all. The mudlarks will have scooped it up by now along with whatever else they could steal from the bastard's body. God, when I think of what that animal might have done to her if I hadn't been there, I—"

It all came back to her then, the drugged milk, her escape from the house, and lastly the man dragging her into the darkened alley. Melanie sat up, the scream she had been unable to utter exploding from her throat.

"It's all right, Melanie." Davies was bending over her, his hazel eyes moving over her face with obvious concern. But rather than being assured, Melanie shrank away from him, cowering against the back of the couch on which she lay.

"You killed him," she croaked, her voice husky from strain. "I saw the knife in his back . . ."

"I had to, my dear, the bastard was going to rape you. It was the only way I could stop him," Drew explained soothingly, his heart twisting at the fear and revulsion he saw on Melanie's face. He hated it that she should look at him with loathing in her eyes.

Melanie shook her head wildly, her dark hair flying about her shoulders. The memory of the blankness spreading across the dead man's face was imprinted on her mind, and she knew she would never forget watching the life flicker and then die in his dark eyes. Not all the Gothics she had read, despite their lurid passages, had prepared her for the brutal reality of such a sudden and violent death.

"Drink this." A snifter of brandy was thrust into her hands, and she dully raised the glass to her lips. The sharp bite of the potent liquor made her choke, but as it hit her stomach, spreading its burning warmth through her frozen limbs, she felt some of the raw panic crowding her subside. As her control returned, so did an awareness of her surroundings, and she raised her head to gaze slowly around the darkened room.

It was small, and if the shabby furniture was any indication, a parlor of some kind. She could see a door in one corner of the room, and a large stone fireplace in the other. A cheerful fire was burning in the grate, casting a warm reddish glow through the room and illuminating the features of the man standing over her.

He was tall, taller even than Davies, with a hard, muscular body that looked somewhat incongruous in his blue velvet evening jacket and cream satin breeches. Thick blond hair was brushed back from a broad forehead, and eyes the brilliant blue of a tropical sea glittered out at her from beneath a pair of straight, tawny-gold eyebrows. Even as part of her mind registered the fact that she had never seen a more handsome man, she also realized she had never seen a more dangerous-looking one.

As if in response to her thoughts, the man's full lips thinned into a cool smile. "I believe your employer has recovered from her fit of the vapors," he said, his eyes flicking over Melanie's head to rest on Davies. "Perhaps you can reassure her we don't mean to slit her throat and dump her in the Thames."

Vapors! Melanie's brows lowered at what she considered a blatant insult. But before she could give voice to her indignation, Davies was bending over her, taking her hand in his as he knelt beside the couch.

"Are you feeling better, Lady Melanie?" he asked, noting her angry expression with an odd sense of relief. If she could look that annoyed, then he knew she was well on her way to recovery. "I don't think you're badly hurt. The wretch didn't have time to do much more than paw you, thank God, but if you'd like we could summon a—"

"You had best think of summoning the constable, you—you murderer!" Melanie exclaimed, flinging aside the comforting touch of his hand. "For you and your fine friend! The pair of you are nothing more than traitors, and I shall see that you hang for your crimes!"

"Indeed?" The other man seemed more amused than cowed by her threats as he sat in the chair facing her. "I'm afraid you might find that a trifle difficult, Lady Melanie, considering your present circumstances."

Melanie's chin came up a notch. It had dawned on her earlier that her position was not a good one. As a woman alone, she knew she stood little chance against two men, especially against a man who had already proven his willingness to commit murder, but she refused to give in. Judging from the sounds coming from the other side of the door, she knew they had to be in some sort of public place, an inn, perhaps, and the knowledge that there were others about bolstered her courage.

"I see nothing wrong with my present circumstances," she replied haughtily, masking her nervousness with an air of disdain. "This is a public inn, after all, and if I were to call out for help, I am sure someone would come to my aid."

"Did anyone come bursting through the door when you screamed?" he asked in a falsely solicitous manner, smiling at her silent glare. "As you can see, I am master of the situation here, and I can assure you that no one will come through that door without my permission, including the constable, should you actually succeed in summoning one."

Melanie hesitated at the arrogant assurance in his voice before turning to confront Davies. "You can't hope to get away with this, you know," she told him angrily, deciding that she was wasting her time trying to reason with the other man. "Mr. Barrymore will know where I am, and you may be very sure both he and my father will not rest until you are tracked down!"

"And how will he know that, my lady?" Drew asked, recognizing a bluff when he heard one. "Are you trying to tell us you left a note?"

"Yes!" Melanie snapped, realizing now that that was precisely what she should have done. In most of the Gothics she'd read the heroines always left some sort of note behind for the hero to find. Unfortunately for her, she had neither a note nor a hero to extract her from her current dilemma, a prospect she found decidedly discouraging. Not that she would let her captors know that, of course.

Drew saw the fear and the bravery in Melanie's brilliant eyes, and it was all he could do not to take her in his arms. He longed to reassure her, but until Sir gave his permission he could not. He would have to cling to his façade until the very end if need be.

"Lady Melanie"—he tried reasoning with her one final time—"I realize this all looks rather bad, but I can assure you that neither Sir nor I mean you any harm. If you—"

"No harm? When you are attempting to ruin my father?" Melanie scrambled to her feet, her small hands closing into tight fists as she bravely faced both men. "Don't take me for that big of a pea goose, Davies ... or whatever your name may be! You are a traitor to the Crown, and if it is the last thing I do, I will see that you and *Sir*"—she cast the other man a fulminating look—"pay for your treason!"

"His real name is Captain Andrew Merrick, lately of the Fourth Mounted Regiment." Sir spoke unexpectedly, regarding Melanie with what Drew now recognized as respect. "And I am his commander. I quite agree with you that there is a traitor on the loose, my lady, but I can assure you it is not Merrick or myself."

"Why should I trust you?" Melanie demanded, bending a suspicious frown on him.

"There is no reason," Sir admitted calmly, folding his arms across his chest. "I have no proof to offer you, no name I can give that would reassure you. Only believe me when I tell you that I act with the highest authority, and that I am just as eager as you to catch the man responsible for the disappearance of those papers from your father's diplomatic pouch."

Melanie slowly lowered her hands. She had no reason to trust either man, and every reason to fear them. Granted they hadn't harmed her, and certainly Merrick's intervention had saved her from a hideous fate, but when all was said and done, she didn't really know either one. And yet . . . she studied the features of the man she knew only as "Sir," noting the unflinching honesty in his sea-blue eyes. The same sincerity was mirrored in Davies's dark hazel eyes, and Melanie knew what her decision would be.

"Very well, Sir," she said majestically, smoothing her muddied skirts about her ankles as she resumed her seat. "I believe you. Now, what are we going to do about it?"

"What do you know of Barrymore?" Drew asked, joining Melanie on the small couch. "How did he come to be in your father's employ?"

"He was recommended to Papa by the Duke of Marlehope," Melanie replied carefully, recalling the day Mr. Barrymore had arrived at their Georgetown home, the letter of introduction from Marlehope in his hand. "His Grace and Papa were old friends, and Papa had mentioned to the duke in a letter that he was in need of an assistant. Mr. Barrymore arrived some seven months later."

"Where had he been before that?" Sir asked, leaning forward to study Melanie's face intently. "Did he ever speak of his past or his family?"

"N-no," Melanie admitted reluctantly, her cheeks paling as a terrible suspicion dawned. "You think it's him, don't you? You think Mr. Barrymore is the one who stole those papers and sold them to the French!"

"As the man himself admits, he *is* the most logical suspect," Drew answered for Sir. "He had access to those papers, and there are several discrepancies in his story that warrant closer investigation."

"Like what?"

"Like the expensive wardrobe he keeps in his closet and the fortune in jewels he keeps hidden in his traveling box," Drew replied bluntly, determined to convince her of the other man's guilt. "There is nothing in his background that would account for such affluence, which means he must have a hidden source of income." His eyes narrowed at the sudden start she gave. "What is it? What are you thinking?"

"When we first arrived in London, he, Papa, and I were sitting in the drawing room discussing the growing hostilities between the Americans and ourselves," Melanie began, nervously moistening her lips with the tip of her tongue. "I remember I said that I could not understand why anyone should want another war, and Mr. Barrymore said it was for profit. He said there were fortunes to be made, and that a man could easily line his pockets if he was of a mind."

"Profiteering." Sir nodded as he considered the matter. "And the scoundrel wouldn't be the first to take advantage of the situation. Yet, if starting a war was his intention, then why didn't he simply give the letter to someone . . . say Calhoun, who would know how to make the best use of it?"

"It was too much of a risk," Drew said after a thoughtful pause. "He would profit only if war actually broke out, whereas the French were probably willing to pay him any price he asked, and in fine English gold." His lips twisted bitterly. "It would seem our Mr. Barrymore is the consummate opportunist."

"Then why are you just sitting here?" Melanie exclaimed, highly vexed by their inactivity. "Go out and arrest him, or whatever it is one does with traitors!"

"Because what we know, and what we can prove, Lady Melanie, are not always one and the same thing," Sir answered calmly. "If we blunder in before we have the proper proof, then Barrymore will go free, and I do not think I need tell you what that would mean for your father."

Melanie bit her lip. Sir was right. If Barrymore was eliminated as a suspect, then that would leave only her father to take the blame. The thought of her proud father standing so accused was anathema to her, and she squared her shoulders proudly. "Very well, then," she said, her violet eyes meeting Sir's steady gaze, "in that case we shall have to get the proof. What can I do to help?"

Drew stirred uneasily at Melanie's words. "I think it might be best if you leave that to Sir and me," he said, exchanging frantic glances with his superior. "We are experts, while you are unskilled in such matters."

"I am not unskilled!" Melanie exclaimed indignantly, casting Drew an angry glare. "I followed *you* here, didn't I?"

"And were almost raped for your pains!" Drew shot back, his cheeks flushing with annoyance at the smile he saw forming on Sir's lips. "You might have gotten lucky in deceiving me this time, but if you try the same thing with Barrymore, you may find yourself in a very uncomfortable position."

"Actually, I think the lady has a point, Merrick," Sir said suddenly, a dimple flashing in his lean cheek. "She did follow you here, after all. My congratulations, ma'am. It was a rather brave and clever thing to do, to pretend to be asleep and then follow Merrick here. However did you think of it?"

Melanie was unable to resist shooting Drew a smug look. "Thank you, Sir," she said, wondering if he ever meant to tell her his real name. "But it really wasn't my idea, you know. I got it out of one of Miss Evingale's books."

"Ah." Sir ignored Drew's muttered imprecations. "I have already had some experience in gleaning useful information from such sources," he said, recalling the havoc Jacinda Malvern had wreaked with the scandalous journals she had penned as Lady X. "You have read many of these books, I take it?"

"Dozens," Melanie admitted happily, delighted that Sir appreciated her value. "And I have several ideas I would be more than happy to share with you if you'd like. What do you think our next step should be?"

There was a moment of awkward silence as Sir and Drew exchanged horrified looks. Drew was the first to recover, his expression forbidding as he studied Melanie.

"*Our* next step is to see you safely home," he said in a most dampening tone. "It should be obvious that you cannot remain here without risking your reputation."

Melanie considered that, then shrugged her shoulders. "I should think having my father tried for treason would be far more ruinous to my reputation than if I should be discovered here," she informed him tartly. "I prefer to stay."

"Your devotion to your father is most commendable, Lady Melanie," Sir began, shooting Drew a silencing look. "But in this case I fear it is sadly misplaced. It would be better for all concerned if you do as Captain Merrick has suggested."

"As he has ordered, you mean," Melanie retorted, her small jaw thrusting forward pugnaciously. "Well, let me tell him and you both that I will not be dictated to by a glorified tin soldier! You forget we are speaking of my father, and I will do whatever it takes to prove him innocent of these ridiculous charges!"

Another uncomfortable silence filled the small room, and again Drew was the first to break it. "Will you?" he asked in a dangerously soft voice, his hazel eyes intent as they rested on her mutinous expression.

"I shall do anything," she reiterated, meeting him glare for glare.

"Including following the orders of a 'glorified tin soldier'?"

A soft flush stole across Melanie's cheeks at the taunting words. She had spoken out of anger, and she found it more than a little disconcerting to have those same words flung back in her face. "I'm not certain I take your meaning," she muttered, shifting uneasily on her chair.

"I mean," he responded with cool deliberation, "that I cannot help but wonder what matters most to you, your father's good name, or your cursed independence."

"How dare you!" she gasped, leaping angrily to her feet. "Who do you think you—"

"Because if it is your father," Drew continued as if she hadn't spoken, "then you'll swallow that aristocratic pride of yours and allow Sir and myself to continue with our investigation. If he is innocent, we are his only hope."

Melanie sat back down with an unladylike *plop*. He was right, curse him, she thought, chewing worriedly on her bottom lip. The evidence against her father was damning, and if he hoped to avoid disgrace, then she had no choice but to do as she was told. The knowledge was far from pleasing, and she made no effort to hide her resentment as she returned his cold gaze. "Very well, Captain," she said, lifting her head with unconscious pride. "What is it you want me to do?"

Chapter Eight

"Nothing."

Melanie blinked at the terse command. "I beg your pardon?"

"I said I wish you to do nothing," Drew repeated, his firm voice revealing no hint of his inner trepidation. He knew Melanie's recalcitrant nature only too well, and he knew if they hoped for her cooperation, he would have to proceed with the utmost caution. "That is to say," he added when it looked as if she might protest, "I don't want you to do anything which might arouse Barrymore's suspicions."

"Yes, that would be disastrous." Sir, who had remained silent during most of their exchange, spoke suddenly, content to follow Drew's lead. "We have been working covertly to trap the scoundrel, but we dare not expose our operation by moving openly against him. At least not at this time. Do you understand?"

"I suppose," Melanie agreed with visible reluctance, "but I still want to help my father. Surely there is something I can do to be of assistance?"

Drew's brows snapped together at her continued obstinacy. It was obvious Melanie was as stubborn as ever. He opened his mouth, about to administer a blistering set down, when a sudden thought occurred to him.

"Actually," he began, striving for a neutral tone, "there is a way you might be of use to us."

"What is it?" She leaned forward, her eyes sparkling with eagerness.

"Despite our best efforts, we've been unable to learn anything of a personal nature about Barrymore," Drew said, taking a chair facing Melanie. "The man is as enigmatic as a sphinx. I was hoping you might be able to remedy that for us."

"But how?" Melanie's brows puckered anxiously. "I have already told you all I know of him."

"Yes, but you could learn more, couldn't you?" he pressed, leaning closer. "You could become better acquainted with him?"

"I could try," she agreed, her mind spinning with possibilities. She had secretly suspected that Mr. Barrymore had a tendre for her, and she had always been careful to maintain a discreet distance between them. Yes, she thought, a slow smile touching her lips, it was the very thing. She would set up a flirtation with him and seduce him into revealing himself to her. It was precisely the sort of thing one of the heroines in a novel might do!

Drew saw only her angelic smile and felt some of the tenseness draining out of him. Thank God the chit was finally seeing the sweet light of reason, he thought, flashing Sir a secret look of male superiority. He was beginning to fear they would have to place her under house arrest in order to carry out the mission.

"Thank you for your help, Lady Melanie," Sir said, rising to his feet. "With luck, we should have this unpleasantness resolved before your father's reputation suffers any irreparable harm. Now, I think we should see about getting you home. It is grown rather late, and we wouldn't want your family to arrive first, would we?"

"Oh . . . no, of course not," Melanie stammered, her cheeks flushing at such a possibility. She stood and faced Sir, uncertain of what her next move should be. The notion of leaving the tiny room and facing a tavern of leering men filled her with fear. The horror of her recent attack was still fresh in her mind, and she dreaded the thought of the darkness that waited beyond the tavern's doors.

Drew saw the uncertainty in her eyes and knew she was remembering what had almost happened in the alleyway. He stepped forward and took her chilled hands in his. "Allow me to escort you home, Lady Melanie," he said softly, his smile reassuring as he gazed down at her. "It would not do for the butler to miss his master's homecoming, you know."

"No, I suppose that would not be at all the thing," she agreed, her trembling lips parting in a brave smile. "We wouldn't want Papa to turn you off without a character."

"I'll see about hiring you a carriage," Sir said, his blue eyes flicking toward Drew. "Shall we say the back door in ten minutes?"

Drew nodded, not taking his eyes from Melanie's face. Unshed tears glittered in her violet eyes, reminding him of the necklace she had worn to Almacks. He remembered how beautiful he had thought her, and how he had longed to voice his appreciation of that beauty. Without being aware of his actions, he lifted his hand and brushed back a tendril of black hair from her cheek.

"Are you all right, Melanie, I mean *really* all right?" he asked in a husky voice, his fingertips gently caressing the curve of her cheek. "You've been through a horrifying experience tonight."

A tremor shook Melanie, but she wasn't certain if the trembling was caused by the memory of the brutal attack or by the gentleness of his touch. His eyes gleamed down into hers, the topaz highlights catching and reflecting the golden glow of the fire. For a moment she forgot everything: the threat to her father, the terror she had just passed through, even her promise to help trap Barrymore; nothing mattered. Nothing save the wild emotion that flooded her body with liquid warmth.

"I am fine, Captain," she said, her soft voice slightly breathless as she stepped back from him. "Although I shudder to think what might have happened had you not been there to save me. Thank you."

"You're welcome," Drew replied, fighting the urge to pull her back into his arms. "But I pray you would not call me by my rank, even in private. My name is Davies, and that is how you must think of me. It could mean my life if you were to slip and call me by any other name."

"Oh, I hadn't thought of that!" she gasped, clapping one hand over her mouth as she stared up at him. "But you're quite right ... Davies. You may rely upon me."

"I know." A tender smile touched his lips. "And if it is any consolation to you, Davies is my middle name."

"That does relieve my mind," Melanie answered, her lips quirking in a smile. "As with Sir, I was beginning to wonder if I would ever know your *real* name."

"No one knows Sir's real name," Drew said unexpectedly, his expression somber. "And I would be most grateful if you would forget having ever met him. He is perhaps the best-kept secret in England."

Melanie, well aware of the need for such men in time of war, was more than happy to give Drew her word. She was only grateful that Sir was more or less on her and Papa's side. She would hate to have such a man as her enemy.

Melanie passed a restless night, awaking from a nightmare-filled sleep to find Mrs. Musgrove sitting at her bedside. When she sleepily asked what she was doing there, the old woman gave a soft chuckle.

"Why, because Mr. Davies told me to, my lady," she said, pressing a glass of water on Melanie. "He told me what had happened to you, and said that you might have bad dreams because of it. And he was right, wasn't he? But you mustn't worry, Lady Melanie, he'll not be letting any harm befall you."

She fell back asleep with that comforting thought uppermost on her mind, and when she next opened her eyes, it was to find her bedroom filled with sunlight. After a quick bath she donned a morning gown of lilac silk and hastened down to join the others at the breakfast table.

Despite the late hour, Mr. Barrymore and the earl were still at home, and after greeting her father with the customary kiss, she sat down beside Mr. Barrymore.

"How did you enjoy last evening, Mr. Barrymore?" she asked, shooting the assistant her brightest smile. "You must tell me everyone who was there and whether or not I was missed."

"Your absence was indeed remarked upon, Lady Melanie," he responded promptly. "Especially by all the young bucks who were hoping for a waltz with you. But all in all I would say that you didn't miss very much. Would you not agree, my lord?" He glanced toward Lord Terrington.

"Quite. The ball was a dashed bore," the earl agreed, digging into his eggs and kippers with obvious gusto. "No one of import there at all. You were quite right to sit it out, my love. I only wish we might have done the same."

"I wouldn't say the night was a total loss," Lady Charlotte objected with an angry scowl. "There was that handsome young man from the Portuguese Embassy who caused quite a stir among the ladies with his flashing dark eyes and his mustachios. What was his name, Mr. Barrymore? You must know, for I saw you chatting with him over by the punch bowl."

"A Senhor Martinez, my lady," Mr. Barrymore replied politely. "He has been in England less than a fortnight, and if my Portuguese serves me, he is having a rather difficult time adjusting to our way of doing things."

"Poor young man, we must invite him for dinner," Miss Evingale exclaimed, her gray eyes taking on a speculative gleam. "Is he like Count Rodrigo, do you think, Lady Abbington? Or more like Count Alvarez?"

"Alvarez," the marchioness replied, bobbing her turbaned head decisively. "He's quite as handsome as Rodrigo, but he lacks the dash and fire of our dear Philippe."

"Rodrigo?" Mr. Barrymore's dark blond eyebrows met in a confused frown. "I must confess the name is not familiar to me. Is he attached to the Spanish Embassy, perhaps?"

"Er . . . he's something of a family friend," Melanie invented, not wishing to explain her grandmother's and companion's idiosyncrasies in front of Davies, although heaven knew he was probably already aware of the fact. She cast a quick glance his way, and thought she detected an amused glimmer in his hazel eyes.

"Did you dance the waltz, Mr. Barrymore?" She turned her attention back to the assistant. "I know there was waltzing; Amelia Hampton was bragging of it at Lady Hertweiler's."

"There was some waltzing," he said with a shrug of his shoulders. "But as a mere assistant to your father, I did not think it seemly that I should dance it. Besides"—he gave her a warm look—"without my favorite partner there, I did not feel the need to take my turn on the floor."

Drew's lips tightened at such blatant flirting. What the devil did Melanie think she was doing anyway, he brooded, leaning forward to pour the earl another cup of coffee. He had only given her the task of learning about Barrymore as a means of keeping her out of his and Sir's way. But he'd never have done so if he'd known this was how she meant to go about it! He should have known she would pull something like this. The first chance he got he vowed to burn each and every one of those silly romantic novels.

"Personally I cannot say I approve of the waltz," Lady Charlotte volunteered, slipping a breakfast bun into her pocket. "It is most unseemly for a man to hold a woman in a shameless embrace—unless they are engaged, of course."

The rest of the meal was devoted to small talk, and Melanie was disgruntled that she had learned so little of value. The only good thing that came of it was that Barrymore did seem to be fonder of her than was proper. Certainly his remark about his "favorite partner" could be counted upon as flirting, and she was eager to press her advantage at the earliest opportunity. With that thought in mind, she set her napkin down and rose to her feet.

"If you will all excuse me, I believe I shall go and change into my riding habit. I feel the need to blow some of the cobwebs from my mind. Would you like to accompany me, Edwina?" she asked, knowing full well that the other woman was terrified of horses.

"R-riding?" Miss Evingale stammered, her hand creeping up to her throat. "Do you mean on a h-horse?"

"Well, I can hardly ride a sheep!" Melanie retorted with a gay laugh. "I haven't had a good ride since coming to London, and I am longing for an invigorating gallop."

"Nonsense, Melanie, stop behaving like a hoyden," her grandmother snapped in her most dampening manner. "Edwina on a horse would be a disaster waiting to happen, and since you cannot possibly ride out alone, I think that is the end of it. Besides, the hairdresser will be here after luncheon to arrange your hair for the ceremony."

"But that won't be for hours yet!" Melanie protested, thrusting her bottom lip forward in a girlish pout. "And I want to ride now. You'll ride with me, won't you, Papa?" She turned toward her father, knowing he could never resist her wheedling tone.

She didn't often engage in such missish behavior, but she felt the situation justified the means.

"Nothing would give me greater pleasure, my dear, but I fear I must be hurrying along," her father said with a heavy sigh. "I have a meeting with the M.P. for Leicester, and I dare not be late. I know"—he brightened suddenly—"Mr. Barrymore can take you, providing he has no objections."

"I would be delighted," Mr. Barrymore assured the earl with a broad smile. "But are you quite certain this will not inconvenience you? I know how important this meeting with Lord Belmont is for you."

"I am sure I can manage his lordship," the earl replied laconically. "The important thing is that Melanie is properly escorted on her ride, else I fear she would strike out on her own. That is what you were planning, wasn't it?" He bent a knowing look on his daughter.

"Papa! As if I should ever be so scheming!" Melanie exclaimed with a guilty blush. She hated the shameless way she was manipulating him, but there was no other choice.

"Ah, it is just as I thought," her father said with a knowing sigh. "Well, at least with Mr. Barrymore to accompany you, I won't need to fear that you will do anything too outrageous. He has a good head on his shoulders."

Melanie excused herself a short time later and went up to her room, where the maid was waiting. After changing into her new habit of sapphire velvet, she clapped her cork hat on her dark curls and went down to wait for Mr. Barrymore. The servants were moving about unobtrusively, and she could see Davies standing beside the front door. Studying his tall, soldierly form, she wondered how she had ever taken him for a mere servant. Miss Evingale was right, she decided with an impish grin; Davies was definitely the stuff of which heroes were made.

As if sensing her gaze, Drew suddenly looked up, his hazel eyes meeting hers. He moved his head imperceptively toward the library, and Melanie nodded in silent understanding. When she was certain no one was watching, she slipped into the room. She hadn't long to wait as the door opened and closed behind a grim-faced Davies.

"Davies, it's going well, don't you think?" she asked, turning to him with an eager smile. "Once we're away from Papa, I am certain I—"

"What the devil do you think you're doing?" Drew demanded with an angry growl, his eyes narrowing with fury as he advanced on her. "I thought you agreed to do nothing that would alarm Barrymore!"

"But—but I haven't," she protested, confused and more than a little annoyed by his apparent animosity.

"And what would you call the way you've been casting sheep eyes at him all morning?" he snapped, his hands dropping to his lean hips. "The man would have to be a dolt not to notice the obvious way you've been flirting with him!"

"I have not been flirting with him . . . exactly," she denied with a slight stammer. The warm gratitude she had been feeling toward him dissolved under a wave of feminine pique, and she met his angry glare with growing defiance. She hadn't been expecting accolades for a job well done, she reminded herself indignantly, but neither had she been expecting such biting criticism.

"Then what were you doing . . . exactly?" he

mimicked her slight hesitation perfectly. "It's certainly not what I instructed you to do."

Her small chin came up in defiance. "You told me to question him, to try to learn something of his past," she reminded him, her tone dripping with honey. "How else am I to do that unless I can speak with him privately? He's hardly likely to blurt out a confession in front of the entire household, you know."

"And he's even less likely to do so to you!" Drew snapped, his mouth tightening in anger. "My God, Melanie, the man is a suspected traitor!"

"Don't you think I know that?" she cried, lifting her chin to meet his gaze. There was a moment of charged silence, but when she spoke her soft voice was devoid of all emotion. "I realize you regard me as a silly female who will only get in the way, and I'm sorry. But I won't let that stop me. I love my father, and there is nothing I wouldn't do to prove his innocence."

Drew turned away from her with an angry oath. The hell of it was that he understood what Melanie was feeling, but that didn't make his job any easier. The evidence was stacked strongly against Lord Terrington, and unless they found more to implicate Barrymore, he would have no choice but to arrest the earl. She was his best hope of trapping the wily spy.

"Very well, Lady Melanie," he said quietly, staring at the rows of books lining the shelves, "question Barrymore, by all means. Should you learn anything, however insignificant, I want you to tell me at once."

Considering that is what she had already planned to do, Melanie inclined her head in cool agreement.

"As you say, Davies," she replied, resisting the urge to salute. "Will there be anything else?"

Drew heard the sweet sarcasm in her voice and hid a smile. "No, that is all, my lady," he answered politely, his hazel eyes dancing with secret laughter. "Enjoy your ride."

Melanie gave him a victorious smile. "Oh, I will, Davies," she promised him in her most dulcet tones. "I will." She was halfway to the door when he called out.

"Lady Melanie?"

"Yes?" She cast him an inquiring glance over her shoulder.

"Be careful."

Hyde Park was all but deserted as she and Mr. Barrymore made their way down Rotten Row, the groom trailing at a discreet distance. But if she thought the absence of others would loosen his tongue, she was soon disappointed, as he proved to be as maddeningly evasive as ever. Not even her most practiced charms succeeded in worming the smallest bit of information from him, and by the end of the ride she was more convinced than ever of his guilt.

Surely such prevarication was as good a proof as anything, she thought, hiding her displeasure as he skillfully sidestepped her question about his schooling. Certainly an innocent man would never go to such lengths to avoid answering a simple question. She was casting about in her mind for some new line of inquiry when she saw two horsemen approaching them at a gallop.

The first man was astride a handsome bay, and she recognized him as Major Richard Dalmire, an elegant young dandy she had met at Almacks. The second man, riding a high-stepping gray, was not known to her, although she thought there was something vaguely familiar about his blond hair and aristocratic countenance. But before she could dwell on the mystery, the two men had joined them.

"Good day to you, Lady Melanie, how pleasant to see you," Major Dalmire said, sweeping his hat from his head and bowing from the waist. "I had no idea you were an equestrienne, else I might have asked you to go riding with me. You looked very much like a young Diana, galloping across our verdant fields."

"You are much too kind, Major," Melanie replied, amused by his effusive praise. "Although I am sure much of the credit must go to my horse; my riding skills are rusty at best." She leaned forward to pat the chestnut-colored mare's arched neck. Her eyes slid to Dalmire's companion, and he was quick to make introductions.

"Lady Melanie, allow me to make you known to my very good friend, Lord Harold Parkinson. Parkinson, I should like to introduce you to Lady Melanie Crawford, the most delightful debutante in London."

"The oldest debutante in London, you mean," Melanie said with a light laugh, extending her gloved hand to Lord Parkinson. His name was still strange to her, but gazing in his deep blue eyes she was struck with the oddest sensation that she knew him. To be sure, she had met many people in her travels with Papa, but she never, ever forgot a face or a name.

"Lady Melanie." Lord Parkinson bowed over her hand, his manner stiffly distant. "A pleasure."

"Thank you." She inclined her head, wondering at his curt manners. Ah, well, she thought, dismissing the matter from her mind, she mustn't become so toplofty that she expected every man she met to fall at her feet. She turned toward Mr. Barrymore, who had been sitting quietly through the exchange. "Major, I believe you have already met my father's assistant. My lord, I should like to present Mr. Cecil Barrymore, he—"

"Introductions are unnecessary, Lady Melanie," Lord Parkinson interrupted, his voice fairly dripping with dislike. "This . . . gentleman and I have already met."

"Oh." For a moment Melanie was nonplused, but in the next the skills she had perfected as her father's hostess came to her rescue, and she was able to give all three men her most charming smile.

"Have you been in London very long, my lord?" she asked, flicking her eyes in the man's direction. "I must say that I find it a most delightful change from Washington, where Papa and I have been living this past year."

"I have been in London for several months, my lady," came the stiff reply as Lord Parkinson continued glaring at them. "As you say, it is a delightful city." He dug his spurs into his horse's flanks, and when the horse danced in protest, he tightened his grips on the reins.

"I am sure you will excuse me, Lady Melanie, but I fear I must be off. My horse is restive, and I would not wish him to become unruly. Good day to you. Come, Dalmire," he called to the major, and then took off at a gallop.

Major Dalmire shot Melanie an apologetic look, then took off after his friend, leaving an uncomfortable silence in his wake. She and Mr. Barrymore turned their horses in the opposite direction of the two men, and after several minutes had passed Mr. Barrymore spoke.

"I suppose I had ought to explain, my lady," he said in a soft voice. "Lord Parkinson is Lord Marlehope's son, and I fear he has little liking for me."

"Indeed," Melanie answered, her heart beginning to pound with excitement. This was the first time Mr. Barrymore had ever mentioned his highborn relation, and she was eager to learn more. "That must make things rather awkward for you," she added encouragingly.

"Not really." He shrugged his shoulders. "We are distantly related at best, and I have never thought to presume upon his lordship's generosity. But unfortunately Lord Parkinson feels differently. He views me as an encroaching mushroom, and never misses the opportunity to put me in what he regards as my place."

"Oh, Mr. Barrymore, how awful for you!" she cried, forgetting her mission as her sympathetic nature took over. "I am so very sorry."

He shrugged again, a sad smile touching his lips. "It doesn't help matters that his father has taken a small interest in my career. Lord Marlehope has been in politics for years, you know, and it was always his fondest wish that his son would one day follow in his steps. Unfortunately the lad has proven to be quite unsuited for the task, and I am told his lordship has had to buy his son's way out of more than one misadventure."

"Ladybirds?"

"And gaming. Lord Parkinson is rumored to be addicted to the faro tables. His debts are said to be astronomical, but I suppose I really shouldn't be gossiping like this." He shot her an embarrassed look. "Family business, you know."

"Of course, Mr. Barrymore, you may count upon me not to tell a soul," she soothed, wondering how much of this she should share with Davies. He did say he wanted to know everything. They continued on their way for another few minutes before she added, "Still, I cannot help but feel sorry for poor Lord Marlehope. How very disappointing it must be for one's only son to turn out to be such a rake and a rattle."

"His only legitimate son, you mean," Barrymore sneered, then a horrified look flashed across his face. "I beg your pardon, Lady Melanie," he said quickly, his agitation obvious. "I should never have said anything so patently untrue; I have no idea what may have come over me. Pray forget the entire matter."

"Consider it forgotten," she said, her mind whirling at the possibilities. The mystery of Lord Parkinson's familiar appearance was solved, she realized, lowering her eyes to hide their excited gleam. Except for some small differences in their height and weight, the two men were close enough in appearance that they could easily be mistaken for brothers.

Chapter Nine

"Are you certain?" Drew gazed down into Melanie's eyes, his hands lightly clasping her shoulders. "Barrymore is Marlehope's illegitimate son?"

"I am positive," Melanie replied eagerly, meeting Drew's intense gaze. "The two of them are as alike as two peas in a pod, and anyone could see that Parkinson detested Mr. Barrymore. Poor Major Dalmire was quite beside himself with embarrassment at his lordship's rudeness."

"But you say Barrymore actually admitted Marlehope was his father?" Drew pressed, his sharp mind seizing on the most pertinent bit of information. He hadn't expected Melanie to learn anything at all, and was amazed that she had uncovered something so vital. This could change everything.

"Well, not exactly," she corrected him, some of her initial excitement fading. She had rushed into the kitchens the moment she had changed out of her muddied habit, eager to share her news with Davies. She found him in the butler's pantry industriously polishing silver, and when she told him she had something important to tell him, he had closed the door behind her.

"Well, what exactly did he say?" Drew asked, frowning at her sudden reservations.

"Well, in one breath he was hinting that Lord Marlehope had an illegitimate son, and in the next he was denying everything. But, Davies, you should see them, they might be twins! They cannot be more than a few years apart in age, and Parkinson was—"

"Then he admits nothing?" Drew interrupted, his hands dropping from her shoulders as he stepped back from her. "Blast it, Melanie, I thought you said that he was Marlehope's by-blow!"

"I said I *thought* he was," she said, trying not to flinch at the crude description. "And I still think so. He looked as if he could have bitten off his tongue when he made that remark, and then he begged me not to mention it to another soul. Besides, something has to account for Lord Parkinson's hatred of him, and he does hate him, Davies; I could sense it."

"Mmm," Drew grunted as he considered what she had said. "I suppose it *is* a possibility," he conceded, rubbing his chin thoughtfully. "And it would definitely explain why Lord Marlehope was so eager to vouchsafe Barrymore's character. Although I still think it sounds like something out of one of Miss Evingale's Gothics," he added, shooting her an accusing glare.

"I shouldn't be so quick to make sport of her if I were you," Melanie retorted, her chin coming up proudly as she met his hazel gaze. "She has proven to be far more astute than either you or I."

"What do you mean?"

"Merely that she has already reached much the same conclusion," Melanie continued, taking smug pleasure in his obvious surprise. "While we were still in Washington, she developed this fancy that he was really the long-lost son of some nobleman or the other, and you would not believe the mischief she caused with her romantic nonsense. At least, I thought it was nonsense at the time, but now I am not at all certain."

"Did Barrymore know of this?"

"One could not help but know, the way she carried on," Melanie laughed, momentarily lost in memory. "Why, I remember once while we were at some Embassy function in Washington she followed him out onto the balcony, where she said he met a man she was certain was his father."

"Why did she think that?" Drew asked, furious with himself that he had dismissed the hen-witted companion without taking the time to question her. If Sir learned he had been so derelict in his duties, he would hand him his head on a platter.

"Because he was so distinguished-looking, she said," Melanie replied, still chuckling. "And because . . ." Her voice trailed off, a look of horror darkening her eyes to deepest purple.

"Because . . . ?"

"Because," she whispered shakily, "they were speaking French."

"What?" he roared, his hands clenching at his side. "My God, Melanie, why the devil didn't you tell me this before?"

"I'd forgotten all about it," she said, shaken at the revelation. "It seemed so silly at the time, just another of her notions. You must know she is addicted to those wretched novels, and she is always mistaking real people for characters in her books.

prised, she certainly had you pegged from the start."

"Me?" He looked faintly horrified at the prospect.

Melanie nodded. "She took one look at you and announced you were simply too handsome to be a *real* butler. Good heavens!" She cast him a horrified look. "You don't think she has said anything to Mr. Barrymore, do you?"

"I hope not," Drew said fervently, shuddering at the thought that they might all be undone by a flighty spinster with more imagination than sense. "Although I should think it most improbable, he seems to give her a wide enough berth."

"That is so," Melanie agreed, relaxing visibly. "Ever since Washington he has been careful to keep a distance between them. And no wonder. Davies, what are you going to do?" She gazed up at him with troubled eyes.

"I don't know," he answered slowly, his natural caution making him reticent. "Sir will have to be informed, plans made, but I think our first step should be to notify Lord Castlereagh that your father is no longer a suspect in all this. Barrymore is our man; I would stake my life on it."

A wave of relief washed over Melanie. Until now she had never dared believe this nightmare would finally end. The knowledge that her papa faced disgrace and even worse had tormented her for so long, she found herself fighting back tears as a great burden fell away. "Thank you, Drew," she whispered, speaking his Christian name for the first time. "Thank you so very much."

"You are most welcome," he said, fighting the urge to press a kiss to the soft lips that were so temptingly close. She was so very beautiful, he thought, his eyes darkening with desire, and the greatest part of that beauty was the loving spirit that blazed so brightly in her jewel-colored eyes. Realizing he had moved closer to her, Drew took a firm rein on his errant emotions and turned away.

"Tell me what else you have learned," he said, picking up a fork and rubbing it carefully with the polishing cloth. "Did he have anything to say about Parkinson?"

Melanie blinked at the abrupt question. Only seconds earlier Davies had been gazing down at her as ardently as any lover; now he was as distant and as cool as a stranger. Hiding her confusion, she quietly repeated everything Mr. Barrymore had told her of the other man.

"I hadn't heard that Parkinson was involved in anything untoward," Drew said when she had finished. "But I suppose I might have missed something." He wisely refrained from mentioning the markers he had found among Barrymore's things.

"Do you think he is blackmailing Lord Parkinson?" She decided that if he could be so businesslike, then so could she. "That would certainly explain his animosity."

"That it would," Drew agreed absently, a faint memory stirring. Hadn't Parkinson accompanied his father to Spain, he mused. If so, then it was more than conceivable that he would have had access to the missing document.

Melanie watched the emotions chasing across Davies's set features and wondered what he was plotting. It was a certainty he would never tell her, she thought, wishing she could insist he confide in her. But she was too aware of the need for secrecy in such matters to make the demand.

"Is Barrymore accompanying you and your father to Court?" Drew asked, deciding the time had come to consult Sir. It would be better for him if the house was deserted when he left, but if not, he supposed he could sneak away. Heaven knew it would not be the first time.

"No," Melanie shook her head. "It will be only Papa, Grandmother, and myself. You must know what Court is like. Are you going to see Sir?" she asked, breaking into an eager smile as realization dawned. "May I come with you?"

"Considering that you will be busy making your bows to the queen and the prince, I should think it most unlikely," Drew said, giving her a slight frown. "Besides, I thought I had made it clear that you were to forget all about Sir. He is never to be discussed, Melanie."

"I do beg your pardon." Melanie bristled at the censure in his voice. She knew she had blundered and was sorry for it, but that did not mean she would allow herself to be scolded like an errant child. She lifted her chin, sending her dark curls cascading down her slender back.

"If there is nothing else you wish to discuss, I believe I will retire to my rooms," Melanie informed him in her most regal tones. "The hairdresser will be here soon, and it would not do for my maid to find me here. Good day, Captain, I will speak with you later." She threw his title out as a challenge, one he acknowledged with a mocking inclination of his head.

"And good day to you, Lady Melanie," he drawled, his lips twitching at the stormy defiance sparkling in her dark eyes. "I trust you will have a pleasant evening at Court. Pray give my respects to their Royal Highnesses." He was still smiling when she stalked out, her small nose held high in the air.

"You were right to come to me," Sir said, his expression serious as Drew concluded his tale. "This is the link we have been searching for. My congratulations, Merrick."

"Thank you, Sir, although the credit is due largely to Lady Melanie's efforts," Drew answered, more than willing to give his imperious lady her due. "She did a first-rate job of reconnoitering."

"So she did," Sir agreed, leaning forward to study his reflection in the cracked mirror as he added the final touches to his disguise. "Although I am sure that was never your intention when you asked her to make up to Barrymore. I gathered you were merely attempting to keep the lady out of harm's way."

"For all the good it did me," came the answering grumble as Drew helped Sir into the scarlet and gold jacket of a Captain of the Guards. "The first thing this morning she was throwing herself at his head like a desperate spinster and insisting that he take her for a ride. It's a wonder he didn't tumble to her at once, for she has certainly never behaved in such a fashion before."

"It may have roused his suspicions, but a man is often vulnerable to women in ways he is never vulnerable to men," Sir said, stroking the luxuriant black mustache that adorned his upper lip. "I have often observed that such men are intolerably vain; he probably accepted Lady Melanie's marked attentions as his due, and thought no more of the matter. There, how do I look?" He turned to Drew for his approval.

The man who stood before Drew was a complete

stranger to him. Sir's dark blond hair and eyebrows had been covered with black dye, giving him the appearance of a dashing brigand, an image that was enhanced by the dueling scar that graced his high cheekbone. Had he not witnessed the transformation firsthand, Drew would never have known this handsome officer for his superior and his friend.

"Like a character out of one of those damned novels," Drew answered, a reluctant smile lighting his eyes. "Am I permitted to ask who you are supposed to be? I hope you have not reenlisted behind our backs."

"Only temporarily," Sir assured him, strapping on the large ceremonial sword that accompanied his uniform. The small stiletto he slipped into his jacket sleeve was far less attractive, but far more deadly. "Allow me to present Captain Stuart Critchley of the Guards, deeply in debt and always eager for a hand of cards." He bowed stiffly.

"Ah, you are going off in search of Lord Parkinson." Drew nodded in understanding. "Do you know where he games?"

"No, but there cannot be that many places where a young lord and his officer friend might go. You did say he was with a Major Dalmire, didn't you?"

"Yes."

"Then I shall just look until I find Major Dalmire. If Parkinson isn't with him, I am sure I can worm his location out of the major with a glass of brandy and a few judiciously lost games. In the meanwhile, I want you to work on a trap for our friend. Have you any ideas?"

"I've been thinking about our Portuguese friend, the one Lady Abbington mentioned Barrymore had been chatting with at some ball or another."

"Senhor José Martinez," Sir supplied, bending to

tuck a small pistol into his shiny Hessians. "My sources tell me he has some interesting acquaintances in the French quarter."

"Yes, and now he is linked to Barrymore, who would doubtlessly accept anything the senhor slips to him with unquestioning gratitude," Drew said with grim satisfaction. "We must make certain it is sufficiently tempting to get Barrymore to lead us to his French contact, and then I shall make it my personal duty to clap the bastard in irons."

Sir glanced up sharply at his words. "Just mind you don't make this *too* personal," he cautioned. "Revenge is a luxury men in our profession can ill afford, and I should hate to see you hurt because you were too blinded by emotion to take proper care."

"You may count upon me to take every precaution, Sir," Drew assured him with an easy smile. "I am too fond of this hide of mine to risk it unnecessarily. But might I advise that you also take care? It would be a great pity if you were to die all rigged out like a play soldier."

"Yes, I dare say I would find it quite embarrassing," Sir answered with a slight smile. "Now, if you will excuse me, 'tis time I was making my rounds. Besides, I am sure you will be wanting to get home before the Terringtons. Tonight is Lady Melanie's presentation, is it not?"

"Yes," Drew replied, a vision of Melanie in her Court dress of white silk with flowers and ribbons decorating the hooped skirts filling his mind. She had never looked lovelier to him, and never more inaccessible.

"Did Barrymore accompany them?"

"To Court? No, but I believe he was planning to

meet some friends elsewhere. Needless to say, I have a man following him," he added sardonically.

"I never had any doubts on that score," Sir told him quietly. "You are almost as cautious as me. But what of the companion? Is there any danger she might be about?"

"No, thank heavens." Drew's reply was heartfelt. "Lady Abbington has arranged for the coach to take her to the palace, so at least I needn't worry that I'll encounter her roaming the halls in search of heroes from her damned Gothics."

Sir chuckled softly. "I think I may have erred in overlooking this particular form of literature," he said, sweeping a cape over his broad shoulders. "It appears to have much to recommend if the quick way Miss Evingale saw through both you and Mr. Barrymore is any indication. Perhaps I should make them required reading for all my agents."

"Or you could start recruiting females with overly active imaginations," Drew agreed, shuddering at the prospect.

"An interesting suggestion, Merrick," Sir said, the look in his eyes frankly speculative as he held open the door for Drew. "Do you think Lady Melanie might be interested in entering my employ? My instincts tell me she would make an excellent operative."

"My God, she would volunteer at once and then demand your most dangerous assignment," Drew muttered feelingly. "You must not even suggest such a thing to her!"

"Oh, your employer is safe enough from me," Sir said, making no effort to hide his amusement. "For the moment."

* * *

Melanie woke with a start, stirring sleepily in her bed. She cast a bleary eye around her, wondering what could have awakened her. She knew it had to be quite late, as it had been well after two when she had finally retired. Supressing a groan, she fell back on the pillows and covered her head. Despite her exhaustion, she knew it would be hours yet before she would be able to close her eyes.

Sighing heavily, she turned on her side, tucking her hand beneath her cheek as she studied the play of light on the wall. Her drapes were partially open and the silver light of the full moon cast an unearthly glow in the room. The presentation had gone well, she mused, smiling as she recalled the events of the past several hours. Much as she had resented the need for such a useless ritual, she had enjoyed herself, and meeting the prince had been a definite treat. He seemed to have singled her out for flirting, something he seldom did with any lady under the age of fifty, and she was aware of the jealous glances being shot her by several of her fellow debutantes.

At the ball afterward she had been swamped with suitors, but even as she had flirted and smiled at them, she found herself wishing that Davies had been there. With his natural grace and power he would make a wonderful dancer, she thought dreamily, picturing herself floating across the floor held tightly in his arms. She wondered if he had ever served with Wellington, for she had heard it rumored that he chose his officers as much for their dancing skills as for their abilities as fighters.

Sir had said he once served with the Fourth Mounted Regiment, which meant that he might have been stationed in Alexandria while she and Papa were there. If he had, she was positive they had never met. Something told her she would not have forgotten his bright hazel eyes, or the unexpected way a smile could light up his face.

Listen to yourself, she thought ruefully, you sound as lovesick as one of Miss Evingale's heroines. Not that she was in love with Drew . . . Davies, by any means, she assured herself anxiously. She admired him for his dedication to his duty, and as he was a handsome man, it was not out of the ordinary that she should find him attractive. But she most definitely did not love him. He was far too autocratic for her tastes, and for all she knew of him he could easily be promised to another.

That bit of speculation brought a swift stab of pain to Melanie's heart, and she swiftly swept the thought aside. No, she was fairly convinced he was neither married nor engaged. Not that it mattered a whit to her, of course, she brooded, tugging the bedclothes about her chin. It was the principle of the matter, and she knew that if she were married, she wouldn't care to have her husband serving in another woman's household. In fact . . . the thought was never completed as Melanie suddenly became aware of the changing pattern of moonlight on the bedroom wall.

Where before there was only the soft glowing light and the shadows cast by the trees in the gardens, she could now see a larger shape moving slowly past. It took a moment for the shape to register in her mind, but when it did, she put a hand over her mouth to cover her scream. The figure creeping stealthily past her window was definitely a man.

Chapter Ten

Fear held Melanie immobile as a thousand possibilities raced through her head. Her first thought was that a thief was trying to break into the house. The recent murders in Wapping Docks, where two families and their servants had been brutally slain in their own homes, were uppermost in her mind, but even as she lowered her hand to scream, another thought occurred to her. What if it were Davies?

He had been waiting up for them upon their return as befitted a proper butler, his manner all that it should be as he took their cloaks and inquired about the presentation. She had studied his face curiously, wondering if he had managed to slip out and see Sir, but with her papa and Lady Charlotte standing in the hallway, there was no way she could ask him. Mr. Barrymore had come in a short time later, and after sharing a small glass of sherry with him and her father, she and her grandmother had retired to their rooms. It had been almost an hour after that before she heard the others coming up the stairs.

If the shape outside her window was Davies, then that meant he had only just now returned from seeing Sir, and she did not think he would thank her if she sounded the alarm. Hadn't he told her repeatedly that secrecy was vital to his mission? On the other hand, she reasoned quickly, if it was not Davies, then it meant someone was definitely up to no good. The balcony that was just outside her window ran the length of the second floor, connecting the various suites. Anyone out on the balcony had only to slide open one of the French doors, and he would find himself safely inside.

Her heart pounding with trepidation, Melanie knew she could not waste another moment on useless speculation. The intruder had already moved past her window and was continuing down the balcony. The knowledge that the rest of her family was sleeping peacefully and unprotected was all it took to send her flying out of her bed, her feet fumbling frantically for her slippers. If some villain thought he could come sneaking into her house unchallenged, then he was about to learn differently.

Slipping her arms into her nightrobe, she padded toward the door, her one thought to reach Davies and warn him of the danger. There was no one about as she cracked open the door and peered cautiously around. She could hear faint noises coming from below, and for a brief moment the terrifying possibility that the man's confederate might already be inside sent a rush of terror through her. Drawing a deep breath, she inched toward the wooden rail and was peering down when a sudden shape appeared out of the darkness.

Despite her best efforts, a small gasp of fright

escaped her parted lips, and she snapped them shut. But it was already too late, for the intruder had stopped and was gazing up into the darkness. She was gathering herself for a blood-curdling scream when a harsh voice called out, "Who is up there? Identify yourself or I will fire!"

Davies! Melanie collapsed against the rail in relief. In the next moment she was pulling herself erect, furious that he should have frightened her so. "It is Lady Melanie," she whispered back, careful to keep her voice from shaking. "I thought I saw something outside my window and was coming to find you. How dare you give me such a fright!"

Drew took the stairs two at a time, the displeasure on his face obvious even in the poor light. "It wasn't me," he hissed, glaring down into her white face. "I was just about to drift off when I thought I heard something up here. How long ago did you see this intruder?" He turned toward her bedroom, the pistol in his hand glinting in the moonlight.

"Not long, less than two minutes ago, I think," Melanie whispered, crowding close to him as he pushed open the door with the palm of his hand. "At first I thought it was a thief, then I thought it might be you, which is why I didn't scream. I didn't think you . . . what are you doing?" She gasped as he crossed the room and opened the door leading out to the balcony. "You can't go out there!"

He cast her an impatient look over his shoulder. "How else do you propose I catch the scoundrel?" he asked sarcastically. "Sit patiently and wait for him to come creeping back? Now, stay here, I can't catch a thief and manage you at the same time." And with that he was gone.

Melanie ran to the door, peeking out into the darkness. She followed Drew's progress as he inched his way along the stone balcony, clutching the gun in his hand. He paused at each door, apparently checking the lock before moving on to the next. Less than two minutes later he was back.

"Nothing," he said grimly, securing the door behind him. "There is no sign of anyone trying to break in."

"But I saw him, Davies," Melanie insisted. "And you said yourself that you thought you heard something!"

"I did," Drew answered, lighting the candle with a flint. "But just because no one was trying to break in, it doesn't mean someone wasn't trying to break out." He turned to face her, his eyes widening in appreciation as he took in her dishabille.

Hair as dark as jet tumbled to her shoulders in a profusion of glistening waves, while deep-violet-colored eyes gazed up at him from an alabaster face. Lips as pink and delicate as a fresh rose trembled with emotion, tempting him to taste their sweetness. His eyes moved lower, taking in the gentle curves revealed by her diaphanous robe. He clenched his teeth, biting back a low groan as desire spread through his veins.

Everything in him was screaming an urgent demand that he take her in his arms and lower her to the tumbled sheets. As a man he had wanted many women, but never with such burning passion, such overwhelming need. He squeezed his eyes shut and swung away from her before his carnal longings overcame his good sense.

"Mr. Barrymore, do you mean?" Melanie asked, trembling with the sweetest of tensions. She was woman enough to see the masculine hunger in Drew's eyes, and wise enough to know there was nothing to be done about it. Despite the pose he was forced to maintain, she knew he was a gentleman, and she knew he would never take advantage of her or the situation. An odd sense of disappointment filled her at the knowledge.

"Yes, I've had a man following him," Drew said, grateful for Melanie's cool handling of the awkward moment that had passed between them. "He may have guessed he was being watched, and thought to slip out undetected. I'd best see if I can pick up his trail."

"You're going after him?" Melanie asked, taking in his disheveled appearance worriedly. He was in his shirtsleeves, his cravat hanging loosely at his throat, and instead of his usual breeches, his legs were encased in a pair of tight buckskins. Dressed like this he looked lean and dangerous, much more like a spy than a butler. She shook her head silently, wondering that she could have been taken in so easily by his deception.

"I have no other choice," Drew said, his heart racing at her warm perusal. He opened the door leading out into the hallway, and after a quick glance to make sure no one was about, he turned back to face her. "I want you to lock this behind me," he instructed her firmly, forcing himself to concentrate on the problem at hand. "If you see or hear anything at all, I want you to scream the house down. Is that understood?"

"Believe me, I will have no trouble on that score," Melanie assured him fervently. "As I said, the only reason I didn't cry out earlier is that I thought it might be you. I didn't think you wanted the whole household to witness your homecoming."

"No, that would have been most awkward," Drew agreed. He knew he was drawing out his departure; more than anything in this world he wanted to stay, and that was why he knew he had to go. "Lock it," he instructed her, departing swiftly before his baser nature got the best of him.

After he had gone, Melanie rechecked the door and then returned to her bed. The candle Drew had lit still flickered brightly in the darkened room, and she cast it a considering look before deciding to leave it burning. It was doubtful she would get any sleep after the fright she had just had, and gazing at the tiny flame gave her an odd sense of security. The flame was still blazing when she fell into an uneasy sleep.

The earl and Mr. Barrymore were gone when Melanie went down to the breakfast table late the following morning. Her grandmother and Miss Evingale had already dined and were waiting for her, their faces both wearing the most somber of expressions.

"Well, the pair of you are certainly looking Friday-faced for such a lovely morning," Melanie said, slipping onto her chair and placing her napkin on her lap. "I do hope no one has died." Drew was nowhere about, and she wondered if it would arouse suspicion if she were to ask after him.

"I would like a word with you following breakfast, Melanie," Lady Abbington informed her coolly, her lips thinning at Melanie's lighthearted mood.

"All right," Melanie answered, not unduly alarmed by her grandmother's apparent anger. The marchioness was often out of sorts in the morning, and she had learned it was best to ignore her sullen moods.

Despite her lack of sleep, Melanie was surprisingly hungry, and she soon made short work of the food brought to her by the attentive footman. She lingered over her coffee, hoping for a glimpse of Drew, but there was no sign of him. Just as she was about to throw caution to the wind and ask that the footman fetch him, her grandmother rose to her feet.

"If you are quite finished now, Melanie, I will see you in the drawing room. There are some things I need to discuss with you. Now, if you please," she added when Melanie hadn't moved fast enough to please her.

"Of course, my lady." Melanie pushed her just-filled coffee cup away and rose to follow the marchioness. Much to her surprise, Miss Evingale accompanied them, a look of grim reproof on her pinched features. She wondered what she could have done to set her mercurial grandmother up in the boughs, and hoped the elderly lady would not ring too great a peal over her head. After last night's alarums, her equanimity was not all that it should be.

As it was, she hadn't long to wonder, for the moment the door had closed behind them her grandmother rounded on her with a vengeance.

"All right, missy," she said, fixing Melanie in an icy violet glare, "I want an explanation, and I want it now. What the devil do you think you are doing dallying with that butler? And don't bother denying it," she added when Melanie's mouth dropped open, "for I saw him creeping from your bedchamber myself!"

Melanie's knees gave way beneath her and she collapsed onto one of the Sheraton chairs. She had been so caught up in her own dreams and desires last night that it had never occurred to her someone might see Drew's departure and draw their own conclusions. What on earth was she to do now?

"I . . . there is a satisfactory explanation for what you saw, ma'am," she began, trying to force her frozen mind to work. If only Drew were here, she thought somewhat wildly, he would know what to do.

The marchioness gave a disbelieving snort. "Oh, I am sure there is an explanation," she snapped, folding her arms across her chest. "But I sincerely doubt I will find it 'satisfactory.' Well? I am waiting."

"There . . . there was a man outside my balcony last night," she began, nervously moistening her lips with her tongue. "I thought he might be a murderer or some such thing and went to get help. Davies had already heard the noises and was up and prowling around. I told him what I had seen, and he came to see what he could find."

"Really?" Lady Charlotte's smile could have curdled milk. "And did he find any sign of this intruder?"

"N-no," Melanie admitted, her usual spirit deserting her in the face of her grandmother's displeasure. "He vanished without a trace. Mr. Davies thought it might be one of the footmen sneaking in after the door was locked."

That was basically the truth, she thought thankfully, or at least as much of the truth as she dared to tell without Drew's express permission. She could only hope that her sincerity would convince her grandmother, otherwise she shuddered to think of what might happen. If her papa learned of this, Drew would be dismissed . . . if not worse, and then they would never trap Mr. Barrymore.

"A footman trying to sneak back into the house through one of *our* suites?" the marchioness sneered, her graying eyebrows descending in a ferocious scowl.

"Oh, cut line, Melanie, how foolish do you think I am? I ain't in my dotage yet, and I would have to be to believe such a Banbury tale! Why, it sounds like something out of one of our novels!"

"Oh, yes, just like *Dark Moor*," Miss Evingale volunteered, pale eyes sparkling with sudden interest. "You remember, Lady Abbington, poor Lady Belinda was stalked by that mad curate who was after Hadrian's treasure. He was right outside her bedroom window, and would surely have killed her if she hadn't screamed for help."

Melanie remembered the book as well, and a bold plot began forming in her mind. It might work, she thought with mounting excitement, and in any case she really had no other choice. If she didn't do something and soon, then all was lost.

"Yes, it is exactly like *Dark Moor*," she agreed, turning to face the marchioness. "Grandmother, do you recall who Cedric is?"

"What? Do you mean that rascally groom who was always in his cups?" Lady Charlotte scowled at her. "Well, of course I do, but I fail to see what some smelly Irishman with a fondness for the grape has to do with all of this. You're trying to distract me, young lady"—an accusing finger was waggled under Melanie's nose—"but don't think I shall be so easily dissuaded! You are risking scandal, and I will not—"

"But Cedric wasn't really a drunkard, was he?" Melanie pressed, leaning forward in her chair to study her grandmother.

"No, he was a Bow Street runner as I recall, but I still don't see what that has to do with anything."

"Well." This was the sticky part. As her grandmother said, she wasn't in her dotage yet, and she would have to be careful not to overplay her hand.

"What would you say if I were to tell you, in strictest confidence, mind, that Mr. Davies is not precisely a butler?"

"I knew it!" Miss Evingale cried, leaping to her feet and clapping her hands with pleasure. "I knew it! Did I not say he was far too handsome and noble to be a mere butler?"

"So you did, Edwina." Lady Charlotte was studying her granddaughter's face for any hint of prevarication. "Are you trying to tell us that Davies is a runner, Melanie?" she asked, still clearly skeptical. "And that he is here on some sort of mission?"

"I know he is acting with full authority of the Crown," Melanie assured her quietly. "But that is all I can say on the matter. You must realize that it could mean his life if anyone were to learn the truth."

"A Bow Street runner, here in our own home." Miss Evingale's eyes were alight with Gothic fervor. "Can you imagine anything so romantic?"

"But why is he here?" Lady Charlotte's eyes were beginning to take on a similar glow, although she was still somewhat uncertain. "And even if he is a runner, it does not explain what he was doing in your bedchamber."

"I told you, I saw someone on the balcony and he was investigating," Melanie said, meeting her grandmother's stare. "As to the other, I am afraid I really am not at liberty to say other than it involves some missing jewels." She stole a bit of a plot from another book, deciding she had nothing to lose at this point. The marchioness and Miss Evingale both seemed to accept her preposterous tale, at least for the moment, and that was all she could hope for.

"Jewels!" Both of the older women echoed, exchanging excited glances. "Do you mean Davies thinks there may be a jewel thief under our roof?" Lady Charlotte sat down, her anger at Melanie forgotten. "I'll bet it's that snake of a Barrymore. I never did trust that fellow; he smiles far too much, and as Shakespeare said, such men are dangerous."

"Er . . . actually, Barrymore is suspected," Melanie said, praying she was not cutting it too close. "But of course, we mustn't say a thing to anyone. He could have confederates anywhere, and we wouldn't wish to imperil Mr. Davies."

"Oh, you may count upon Edwina and me," Lady Charlotte said, straightening her turban with an eager hand. "We know enough to keep our lips buttoned. "Don't we, Edwina?"

"Indeed we do, your ladyship," Miss Evingale answered with alacrity. "And pray tell Mr. Davies that he may rely upon us to render him whatever aid he may require! But there is only one thing I do not understand."

"What is that?" Melanie asked warily.

"How did you learn he was a runner?" Miss Evingale queried with a puzzled frown. "If he was operating sub rosa, however did you learn the truth? I'm certain he wouldn't have simply confided in you."

Of all the times for her witless companion to ask an intelligent question, Melanie seethed, searching her brain for some answer with which to fob her off.

"Goose!" Lady Charlotte gave Miss Evingale an offended glare. "She deduced it! As you say, he is far too handsome and mysterious to be an ordinary servant. What else would he be but a runner?"

"That is so," Miss Evingale agreed with a sigh. "He is the veriest hero; I have always said so."

"And I knew something was amiss the moment I clapped eyes on him," Lady Charlotte said smugly. "We Abbingtons are nothing if not observant. I dare say I would have tumbled to the truth any day now if I had thought about it."

"I am sure you would have, Grandmother," Melanie said soothingly, almost drooping with relief. "And now that I have your word that you will tell no one, not even Papa, what you know, I believe I shall go up to my rooms. We are dining with the Hampfields this evening, are we not, ma'am?"

"What?" Lady Charlotte blinked at the sudden change in conversation. "Oh, yes, so we are. But really, Melanie, I have dozens of questions to ask you about Davies. You cannot expect us to go blithely about our way as if nothing has happened."

"Ah, but that is precisely what we must do," Melanie was quick to reply. "Davies was most emphatic on that point. He says that it is imperative that we all behave as normally as possible. We wouldn't wish Mr. Barrymore to become suspicious, would we?"

"No, we would not," Lady Charlotte declared decisively. "Davies is quite right; we shan't alert the wretch that we are on to him. You may inform Davies that we shall be the souls of discretion."

"Thank you, my lady," Melanie said, careful to keep any hint of irony out of her voice. "I am sure he will be pleased to hear it."

"You did *what*?" Drew stared at Melanie as if she had taken leave of her senses. "My God, Melanie, please tell me you are joking!"

"I only wish I were," she replied, slumping lower in her chair. She and Davies were sitting in her father's study, where she had arranged to meet him before the family was to leave for the evening. He had entered the room through the hidden door, a secret she had found most intriguing.

"But a Bow Street runner?" He ran a hand through his dark hair, his hazel eyes shimmering with frustration as he glared at her. "Why didn't you just tell them I was a spy and be done with it?"

"I told you, there was nothing else to be done!" Melanie snapped, her chin coming up defiantly. She was feeling hard pressed by the events of the past two days, and Drew's cold criticism made her burn with resentment. "I had to do something," she continued in a bellicose voice. "Grandmother had seen you leaving my room and was fit to do murder. She would have gone to Papa, and then where do you think you would have been? Saying you were a Bow Street runner may not have been the most clever thing I could have done, but it was all I could think of at the moment."

Drew gazed down into her angry face another moment and then turned away with a heavy sigh. "I'm sorry, Melanie," he said quietly, crossing the room to stand before the fireplace. "I shouldn't have snapped at you like that. You're right, you did the only thing you could, and I thank you. It would have been disastrous if I had been dismissed from my post."

"That is what I thought," Melanie agreed, relieved he was no longer angry with her. "When Miss Evingale mentioned that book, I realized she was offering me the perfect excuse, and I seized it with both hands."

"A tactical decision I am sure Sir would support," Drew said with a slight smile, envisioning his response when he learned of this latest fiasco. "He is a great believer in using whatever tools come to hand."

"Speaking of Sir, have you been to see him? Did you tell him about Mr. Barrymore?" she asked, happy that the awkward moment was behind them. "Was that him creeping past my window last night? Did you follow him?"

"Which question shall I answer first?" Drew asked, hiding his uneasiness behind a smooth smile. He had been an agent for too many years to confide in anyone comfortably, and he honestly felt Melanie was best left out of things. If Barrymore ever suspected she was a part of this . . . he refused to consider the possibilities.

"Did you tell Sir about Barrymore?" she asked, deciding that was the most important thing for the moment. "When is he going to have him arrested?"

"Soon." He felt safe telling her that much, at least. "We are readying a trap now, and the moment he takes the bait, we shall have him. Your father's name will be cleared, Melanie, that much I can promise you."

Melanie said nothing, surprised at how bereft his words made her feel. This is what she had been praying for since she had first heard that woman gossiping at Almacks. Why then did she want to burst into tears at the very thought? Melanie's heart knew the answer to the question, but her head refused to acknowledge the unhappy truth.

Chapter Eleven

"Ah, Melanie, dearest, there you are," the earl greeted Melanie as she returned from making her afternoon calls. "I was wondering if I might have a word with you."

"Of course, Papa," she replied, surrendering her pelisse and bonnet to the footman. A quick glance around the hall showed that Drew was nowhere to be found, and she wondered if he had slipped away to visit Sir. In the two weeks since her presentation, he had spent more and more time away from his duties, often returning with a grim look on his face. She had the feeling something momentous was afoot, and she wished he would confide in her.

"Where are your grandmother and Miss Evingale?" Lord Terrington queried as he led her to the Duchess's Room. "Did they not accompany you to Lady Wilton's?"

"Yes, but they thought to visit the lending library," Melanie explained, taking a seat on the gold settee. She cast a fond look about the sunlit room, thinking how much she had grown to love it. She would miss it once they were back in the country. In fact, she thought unhappily, there were a great many things she would miss.

"I have some news for you, my dear, which I think you might find of interest," her father began without preamble, his eyes glowing with eagerness. "I have been given a new post."

"Papa, that is wonderful!" she exclaimed, leaping to her feet and throwing her arms exuberantly about his neck. "Where are we going? And when shall we be leaving?"

"Not for a good while yet," the earl chuckled, returning her effusive embrace. "And as to where, I am afraid that has yet to be decided. All I can tell you is that the Foreign Secretary himself took me aside to tell me not to get too settled in my new position, as he had other plans for me."

"Oh, Papa, I am so happy for you," Melanie replied, blinking back tears of joy as she resumed her seat. Sir must have contacted Castlereagh, she realized, impressed by the power wielded by Drew's enigmatic superior. Castlereagh was a man not easily led.

"There, did I not tell you not to worry over those silly rumors?" Lord Terrington teased, feeling magnanimous now that the danger had passed. "All worked out in the end just as I said it would."

"If you say so, sir," she answered with a knowing smile. "But surely his lordship must have given you *some* sort of hint about your next assignment. What did he say?"

"Only that he had other plans for me," he answered, folding his hands across his stomach as he regarded Melanie with loving amusement. "There was a mention of a more felicitous climate, quite unlike what we endured in America, but other than that the viscount was as coy as a maiden. So what do you think, eh, my dear? Ready to follow the drum with your poor old father?"

"More than ready," she replied, forcing a light note into her voice. "Only tell me when we are to leave and I shall begin packing at once."

"It is odd, but I had rather hoped to see you married by now, or betrothed at the very least," the earl said in a thoughtful manner. "It was the reason I insisted you be presented, after all. Is there not some young man who has caught your fancy?" He studied her hopefully.

"Oh, Papa." Melanie shook her head at him, knowing she could never tell him the truth. "We have rubbed along quite well together all these years. Whyever should I wish to trade that for a life of dull respectability?"

"There is nothing dull about respectability, Melanie," he rebuked her sternly, thinking of the scandal that had dogged him so recently. "But you still have not answered my question. Is there not some man in the whole of society who has caught your interest? It's not as if you hadn't taken, after all. Our house has been filled with beaus since you made your bows."

"Corinthians and fops." She dismissed her suitors with a wave of her hand. They had all been charming and attentive, but compared to Drew they were all shallow little boys, and she could not find it in herself to give them even the slightest encouragement. "Or else they were fortune hunters," she added, remembering some of the other men who had danced attendance upon her.

"Ah, you are referring to Sir Melvin," the earl said with a brisk nod. "Well, you needn't have worried I would even consider his offer! Not only were the man's pockets to let, but he is a younger son with no claim to a title. As my daughter, I expect you to aim a trifle higher than that."

"Papa!" Melanie was scandalized by her father's sudden display of snobbishness.

"Well, I am sorry, my dear, but we must live in our world as it is, not as we would like it to be," he replied in his thoughtful manner. "With things as they were, I wanted the comfort of knowing that you would be protected, whatever might happen. As my daughter and my only heir, you will be inheriting a substantial fortune as well as my name. Is it small wonder that I should want the best for you?"

"Yes, but the best need not include an empty title! Just because a man is accepted in polite society, it does not mean he is a gentleman!" she replied, thinking of Mr. Barrymore. The man had ingratiated himself with half the hostesses in London, and when she thought of how he was deliberately using both her father and herself to further his own ambition, it made her long to scratch his eyes out. She could not wait until Drew exposed him for the villain that he was.

"I see."

Her father's contemplative voice brought Melanie's head up in alarm. "And what is that supposed to mean?" she asked warily.

"Only that you have been spending a great deal of time with Mr. Barrymore these last weeks," the earl replied, his glance frankly speculative as he studied her. "And the two of you have always been rather close. In Washington he was your favorite dancing partner."

"In Washington he was the only one who could

dance without tramping all over my feet!" she replied with decided heat, horrified by her father's line of questioning.

"Granted, but you cannot deny that you have been setting your cap at him these last few weeks," the earl replied doggedly. "What of the day you teased him into riding with you? And only last evening you danced two sets with him at the Embassy's ball. What else am I to think?"

"Well, certainly not that I am romantically interested in him!" Melanie answered quickly, wondering how she could extract herself from this mess. The only reason she had danced with Mr. Barrymore at all was to alleviate any suspicions he might have. And to learn what he was doing chatting with that Senhor Martinez, she thought, remembering how secretive the two of them looked whispering in the corner. She would have to tell Drew what she had seen.

"Are you quite certain you do not have a tendre for him?" Her father was regarding her with a worried frown. "He has been an excellent assistant, but if I thought even for one moment that you were interested in him, then I would have no choice but to dismiss him from my service. A man of his questionable background is hardly the type of man I would allow to pay court to my only daughter."

"I can assure you, Father, that I haven't the slightest affection for Mr. Barrymore above the common," Melanie said, meeting her father's steady gaze. "I regard him as a—" She stopped abruptly, her brows puckering in a frown as she considered his last words. "What do you mean, a man of his questionable reputation?"

The earl colored at Melanie's perceptiveness. "I beg your pardon, my dear, and ask that you forget that last unfortunate remark," he said, looking faintly embarrassed. "It was most unkind of me."

"But what do you mean?" Melanie persisted, leaning forward on the settee to study her father's face. "Has it anything to do with his being Lord Marlehope's bastard?"

"Then you know?" Her father was obviously scandalized. "But how could you? I only recently learned of it myself, and the duke swore me to secrecy. Did Mr. Barrymore say anything to you?"

"Hardly," she answered, nibbling on her lip as she debated what to tell her father. Drew had sworn her to secrecy, but since he had already learned the truth of Barrymore's birth, she could see no harm in telling him more. After a moment's consideration she related the circumstances of that morning ride she had taken with the assistant, including the uncomfortable encounter with Lord Parkinson.

"I would never have suspected it had I not seen the two of them together," she concluded, confident that she had done the right thing. "And after Mr. Barrymore's bitter comment, well, I would have to be a pea goose not to have tumbled to the truth. What did the duke say to you?"

The earl shifted uncomfortably in his chair. "I told you, my dear, His Grace swore me to secrecy, and in any case, it is hardly the type of thing a gentleman would discuss with his unmarried daughter."

"Oh, please, Papa, I am hardly a green girl!" Melanie gave him an exasperated look. "Besides, I do not understand why the duke even sent Mr. Barrymore to you at all if he is so ashamed of him."

"But that is just it. Lord Marlehope didn't send the wretch to me!" he blurted out, feeling faintly harassed. "In fact, he wasn't even in Madrid when my letter arrived. It was his son, Parkinson, who intercepted my letter and then decided to send Barrymore to America when I mentioned I had need of an assistant. He was probably trying to avoid a scandal by shipping him safely across the Atlantic. And in all fairness to Barrymore, I really cannot fault his performance. As I have said, he is an excellent assistant."

Oh, Papa, if only you knew, Melanie thought, eager to relay what she had learned to Drew. Perhaps now there would be enough proof to arrest the scoundrel before he ruined everything. It wasn't as if they had all the time in the world, after all. The season would be over at the end of the month.

"You must promise me not to tell anyone," her father instructed her in a stern manner. "Mr. Barrymore may not be all that he should be, but I will not have him gossiped about. Is that clear?"

"Oh, yes, Papa," Melanie answered, casting her eyes down demurely. "Quite clear."

They were to spend a quiet evening at home that night, in order to rest for the ball being held at Clarence House the following evening. The ball was for diplomatic personnel returning from a successful mission to Russia, and with her father's return to grace, they had received an invitation only yesterday. Melanie sat at her place, picking at her food as she debated how to get Drew off for a few minutes of private conversation.

He had arrived at the house to help serve dinner, and there was no time to take him aside. She had tried shooting him meaningful looks, but he ignored them, serving the earl his meal with what she regarded as unwarranted devotion. Finally in frustration she decided she could wait no longer and set her fork down.

"Mr. Davies," she began, making her voice as haughty as possible, "I would like to see you in my father's study after dinner, if you please. There is a small problem with the footman I should like to discuss with you."

Drew's eyebrows rose not only at her superior tones, but at the bold way she had made her announcement. It was obvious the little minx was up to something, and with the plan already set into motion, he could not afford any distractions at this point.

"Very well, my lady," he said, inclining his head politely. "I shall place myself at your disposal."

"Really, Melanie, if there is some problem with the staff, you might let me handle it," Lady Abbington said, shooting an angry scowl at her granddaughter. "I know you are used to being mistress in your own household, but may I remind you that I am your father's hostess? If there is something amiss, I should be the one to speak to the butler."

"I know, Grandmother." Melanie gave the marchioness a soothing smile. "But you have done so much already that I do hate to bother you with what is really a trifling matter. Besides, did you not say you and Miss Evingale meant to finish *Dark Moor* tonight?" She waggled her eyebrows meaningfully.

"Eh? *Dark Moor?*" Lady Abbington blinked in confusion. "But haven't we already . . . oh!" Her brow cleared as if by magic. *Dark Moor!* "Yes, you are quite right, my dear. Edwina and I are longing to finish that book. Is that not so?" She addressed the question to the companion, who was looking on with wide-eyed eagerness.

"Indeed we are, your ladyship, indeed we are,"

she replied, all but rubbing her hands in glee. "There is nothing like a good Gothic, I have always said."

"Well, mind you, don't tie up my study too long, my dear," her father said, finishing the last of his mutton. "There are some new dispatches I am to examine before they are released to the House of Lords."

"Would you like any assistance, my lord?" Mr. Barrymore inquired, his manner solicitous. "I have hardly had a thing to do in these last weeks, and I am beginning to feel I am not earning my keep."

"What nonsense, my boy," the earl replied with a hearty laugh. Despite what he knew of the lad's birth, it was obvious he was determined not to hold it against him, and the smile he gave him was a genuine one. "You have been of more help than you realize. Besides, did you not tell me you were invited for cards at a friend's club?"

"Yes, but my plans can always be changed if you should have need of me," Mr. Barrymore said with a fawning smile. "And as I am a poor card player, I dare say it might be better for my pocket if I did stay at home."

"Nonsense, Mr. Barrymore, a good game of chance never hurt anyone," Lord Terrington assured him with a low chuckle. "Just mind you are in at a decent hour, as we will have a full day ahead of us what with the debating session and then the ball at His Highness's house."

Drew poured the earl fresh coffee as the two men continued discussing politics in an animated fashion. He found Barrymore's remarks about his lack of card skill to be most interesting in the light of what Sir had learned. It seemed that the man was a cardsharp who had won enough markers from

Lord Parkinson to place the earl firmly in his pocket. That was one hold over Marlehope's head, which doubtlessly explained why the duke had been so eager to fob him off on Terrington. The other hold was his illegitimacy, which although yet to be proven, was unquestionable. As Melanie had said, Parkinson and Barrymore could easily be taken for brothers.

Thinking of Melanie brought to mind her bold demand to see him in the study. What maggot did the little hellcat have in her brain this time, he wondered, shooting her a thoughtful glance. From looking at her now, dressed in a demure gown of soft cream-colored satin trimmed with bunches of violets, one would think her innocent as a lamb. But he knew better, of course. Melanie was about as innocent as a loaded musket!

After dinner Melanie sailed grandly into the study, her heart beating with eagerness. She had barely settled in her chair when there was a knock at the door and Drew stepped inside the room.

"Yes, your ladyship, what is it I can do for you?" he asked, bowing stiffly.

Melanie leapt up from her chair and hurried to his side. "Drew! You are never going to believe what I . . . umph!" She gasped as he clamped his hand over her mouth.

"Quiet, you little fool!" he instructed her harshly, pulling her away from the door. "Hasn't it occurred to you that Barrymore might be listening?" He pushed her none too gently back onto her chair and went to press his ear against the door. Satisfied there was no one there, he turned away, his eyes icy with displeasure as he studied Melanie sitting stiffly in her chair.

"I want to know what the devil you think you

172

are doing," he said, folding his arms across his chest as he confronted her. "How are we to keep my identity a secret if you persist upon arranging these little assignations?"

"Assignations?" she gasped, her eyes narrowing with indignation. "How dare you, sir! And how else am I to arrange to speak with you, I should like to know!"

"There is no reason at all you should need to speak with me," Drew answered harshly as he took a chair facing hers. He had just come from seeing Sir, and the knowledge that this would be all over in a matter of days had left him feeling decidedly raw. In the few weeks he had come to know Melanie, he had grown surprisingly close to her, and the thought of never seeing her again filled him with grim despair.

"Really?" She gave him her sweetest smile. "Not even the news that Marlehope admitted to my father that Barrymore is his illegitimate son?"

"What?" Drew was on his feet again, gazing down at Melanie in astonishment. "When? What did he say?"

Much as she would have liked to have him beg for every tidbit of information she possessed, Melanie knew the situation was too important for such antics. But that did not mean she didn't take pleasure in drawing out her tale as long as possible. By the time she had concluded, Drew was pacing back and forth angrily.

"Then it was Parkinson who sent Barrymore to your father?" he asked, coming to a halt beside her chair. "He had access to the duke's diplomatic pouch?"

"So it would seem," she answered, studying his shuttered expression thoughtfully. "Papa thinks it was because Lord Parkinson wished to avoid scandal by shipping Mr. Barrymore to us, but I think it has to be more than that, especially since we know him to be a traitor."

"A traitor who likes to play both ends against the middle," Drew answered grimly, rubbing the back of his neck with his hand. "Well, at least we know now how he came to be in America. All that remains now is to learn whether he knew of the dispatches' existence before or after he came to your father. If it was before . . ."

"Then that would implicate Lord Parkinson," Melanie finished for him, her eyes beginning to sparkle. "Now that I think of it, he served in his father's absence while His Grace was called home for an emergency. Do you think Mr. Barrymore was blackmailing him?"

"It's a possibility," Drew admitted, the gambling markers again uppermost in his mind. The total was well over fifty thousand pounds, a rather steep amount even for a young lord who would one day inherit a wealthy dukedom. If Barrymore brought pressure to bear, it wasn't inconceivable that Parkinson might have crumpled, although he hoped such was not the case. From what Sir had said, the lad had much to recommend him, and it would be a great pity that he should have to pay for his half brother's greed.

"More than a possibility if you ask me," Melanie sniffed, annoyed by Drew's lack of enthusiasm. Then she remembered the other thing of import she had to relay to him, but before she could speak, a sudden noise from behind the drapes brought them both whirling around.

"Well, a fine Bow Street runner you turned out

to be!" Lady Charlotte said, stepping out from the hidden door.

"G-Grandmother!" Melanie stammered, pressing both hands to her chest in order to calm her wildly beating heart. "Where did you come from?"

"From the secret passage, of course," the marchioness replied, casting Drew a haughty look. "It's a little late for that, don't you think?" she asked querulously, indicating the pistol he held leveled at her. "Had I been a real villain, the two of you would have been as dead as a pair of mackerel by now!"

"Did you tell her about the secret passage?" Drew demanded as he stuffed the pistol back into the waistband of his trousers. The shock of the countess's sudden appearance coupled with the anger he was still feeling left him spoiling for a fight, and he was just looking for a reason to explode.

"Of course not," Melanie snapped back, as ready for battle as was he. "How could I? I didn't even know about it till now!" She turned to face her grandmother. "How did *you* learn of it?"

The countess gave a loud sniff. "Don't be absurd, Melanie," she said in her most dampening manner. "Where there are jewel thieves and Bow Street runners there are always secret passages. We simply looked until we found it. Which reminds me, Davies, or whatever your name may be, you really must speak to Lord Marchfield about that passage. It is quite deplorable. Not a skeleton or a cobweb to be found. We were most disappointed."

"We?" Drew managed, a sense of inevitability overwhelming his anger.

As if in answer to his question, Miss Evingale appeared in the opening, her cheek adorned with a smear of dirt. "You were quite right about his hat box, my lady," she said, rushing forward to offer the items she held cupped in her hands to the marchioness. "I found these in the lining." She poured a glittering array of jewels into Lady Abbington's hands.

"Ha! Well, you have him now, Davies!" she gloated, picking out the gold ring Drew had already examined. "Do you see this? That is the Duke of Marlehope's crest, I'd know it anywhere! And I know full well he would never willingly part with it. Well, what are you waiting for? Go clap him in irons and take him off to Newgate! That is your job, is it not?" A gray eyebrow was raised haughtily.

"So it is, my lady." Drew was horrified to find himself choking back laughter. The situation was about as grim a one as he had ever faced; with his whole mission threatening to explode about him, and yet . . .

"That is excellent proof, Grandmother, and I quite applaud the bravery with which you and Miss Evingale have gathered the evidence!" Melanie said, leaping to Drew's rescue. She could well understand his dilemma, for it was all she could do not to burst out laughing at the absurdness of their situation. She was willing to bet it was the first time he had ever been routed by a dowager and a spinster, she thought, biting her lip to keep from smiling.

"Yes, it was rather brave of us, wasn't it?" Lady Charlotte preened at Melanie's words. "Not that we ever wavered in our duty, mind. Which brings us back to you, sir." She swung around on Drew. "I insist you arrest that blackguard before he robs us all blind!"

"That is easier said than done, my lady," Drew began, calling upon his training to regain control. "For you must know that I am a . . . er . . . junior operative, and I really cannot make an actual arrest without my superior's permission. But with this kind of evidence"—he indicated the jewels still clasped in the marchioness's hands—"I dare say that permission will soon be forthcoming. My thanks to you both. England is in your debt."

Judging from the grins on both women's faces, Drew realized he must have said the right thing, and his shoulders sagged in relief. Sir was right, he decided, mentally wiping his brow. These Gothics definitely contained valuable information, and the first chance he had, he meant to read a shelf full of them. But he was not out of danger yet, and assuming a conspiratorial smile, he leaned forward.

"Naturally we must return these to our suspect," he said with a confiding smile. "We would not wish our rat to know we are on to him and smell the trap, now, would we?"

"Yes, quite right," the marchioness agreed with a cool nod. "There is more than enough time to recover our property, I suppose, for some of these rings look rather familiar now that I think of it. Come, Edwina." She turned toward the door still hidden behind the drapes. "Time to go skulking about again!"

"Oh, yes, your ladyship!" Miss Evingale gushed, hurrying forward to join Lady Abbington in the passage. "And this time perhaps we might investigate the library? I'm sure there must be treasure hidden in there as well." And the door swung shut behind them.

It wasn't a moment too soon, for Drew and Melanie exchanged glances and then broke into laughter. "My God, was ever an agent so bedeviled?" Drew asked when he could finally draw breath. "I never thought the day would come when a woman in her eighties would take me by surprise!"

"And what of me?" Melanie demanded, laughter lighting her jewel-colored eyes. "You told me about the hidden door, sir, but you neglected to mention it was connected to a secret passage. Does it run the entire length of the house?"

"Most of it," he admitted, still chuckling. "And as for not telling you, my lady, might I remind you that I am an agent? We must have our secrets, you know."

"Mmm, and you seem to have more than most," she said, tossing back her head and smiling up at him. A tendril of hair fell across her flushed cheek, but before she could brush it aside, Drew's hand was already there, his fingers warm on her face.

The witticism he was about to utter withered on Drew's lips as his eyes met Melanie's. They were as deep a purple as a summer's twilight, and as warm and inviting as a roaring fire. Her cheeks were pink with laughter, and her soft lips warm and moist. As if acting on their own accord, his fingers moved from her cheek to her lips, brushing them with reverent care.

Melanie trembled at his touch, and at the fire she saw burning bright in his light hazel eyes. Emotions she had never experienced tore at her, and she was unable to resist their power. She slowly lifted her arms, her eyes never leaving Drew's as she circled them around his neck. "Drew," she whispered softly, and it was all the invitation he needed.

His lips met hers in the most fiery of kisses, his mouth warm and demanding as it moved against hers. She responded with eager passion, her lips parting to accept the delicate touch of his tongue.

The sensation was almost overwhelming, and she cried out against the rapture.

"Melanie, oh, God, Melanie, how I have longed for this," Drew groaned, pressing ardent kisses on the curve of her cheek. "You are so beautiful, so very beautiful. You make me burn from wanting you!"

His words inflamed the desire burning in Melanie, and she tightened her hold, pressing against him until she could feel his heart pounding in rhythm with her own. "Drew, you make me feel so alive!" she said, burying her fingers in his soft brown hair. "What am I going to do?"

He closed his eyes at her words, a sharp thrust of anguish momentarily killing his passion. At that moment he knew he loved her, and knew, too, that he could never have her. Shuddering at what the effort cost him, he put her firmly away from him.

"I will have to go to Sir and tell him about Barrymore," he said, his voice still husky from unslaked desire. He prayed she was too innocent to recognize it, or the other signs of his arousal, although there was little he could do about it. For now it was taking everything he possessed to even think in a rational manner.

"I want your promise that you will give Barrymore as wide a berth as you can," he continued roughly, turning away from her. "Our trap is set to be sprung tomorrow at the Prince Regent's, and nothing must interfere. Barrymore may become dangerous when he realizes he has been caught, and I don't want you getting in the way. Is that understood?"

"Y-yes," Melanie stammered, stunned by the abrupt change that had come over Drew. He had been as ardent as she had dreamed he would be, and she found it difficult to understand how he could go from a passionate lover one moment to a cold-blooded spy the next, unless the embrace had meant less to him than it had to her, she thought, the lowering realization making her pale in distress.

"I'll do all that I can, Captain," she said, forcing her voice to remain as cool as his. "But it might be rather difficult considering we will be sharing a coach. My father won't be in any danger, will he?" she added as the thought suddenly occurred to her.

"No." Drew heard the coldness in her voice and knew he had hurt her. He longed to take her back in his arms and bring the light back to her eyes, but for now the demands of duty were more pressing. Even if he could never call her his own, he was determined to clear her father's name once and for all. "We've arranged for Martinez to slip him a false message out on one of the terraces, and then the moment he is alone we will move in on him. It will all be done very discreetly, believe me."

Melanie believed him. If she had learned anything of Drew, it was that he always did what he set out to do. There was an air of ruthlessness about him that was unmistakable, but dangerous as he was, he lacked Sir's deadly aura. It was an odd realization, and one she dismissed at once. A discreet glance at the clock on the mantel showed that she and Drew had been closeted alone for almost twenty minutes, and she imagined her father would be chomping at the bit to get at his papers.

"I suppose we should give Papa back his study," she said with commendable calm. "And besides, we wouldn't want to raise any suspicions. Good night, Davies, and kindly give Sir my best. Will he be there for tomorrow's festivities?"

"Perhaps," Drew edged, relieved she was making it easy for him to leave, but annoyed at the same time. "But I wouldn't look for him if I were you. He will doubtlessly be in disguise."

"Of course." She inclined her head mockingly. "I might have expected as much. Good evening, then." She strode past him, her head held proudly in the air. She had almost made it to the door when she stopped.

"Davies?"

"Yes, my lady?" He regarded her cautiously.

"Be careful."

Chapter Twelve

"Are you certain this will work?" Drew asked, studying Sir worriedly. "It all sounds too damned easy; I don't like it."

"Things need not always be as complicated as we make them," Sir answered after considering Drew's objections. "And often the simple approach is the best. We know that Martinez has acted as a courier for Barrymore in the past, so there is no reason to think he will suspect him now. Relax, Merrick, it will all turn out in the end."

"Maybe," Drew conceded, lifting the snifter of brandy to his lips, "but I still don't like it. There's too much that can go wrong, and there would be Melanie and her father caught in the middle. You and I both know how desperate a man can be when there is no way out."

"But Barrymore is not an agent," Sir reminded him, his mouth twisting with derision. "He is nothing more than an opportunist and a thief who would doubtlessly steal the shillings off a dead man's eyes.

We have taken down bigger and more dangerous men, Merrick, so rest assured that your employer and her father will come to no harm."

Drew said nothing, allowing himself to be convinced by Sir's unwavering faith in himself. And he was right, Drew decided, shifting back in his chair and crossing his feet as he studied the flames in the fireplace. Barrymore would be too busy smacking his lips in anticipation of the French gold he was expecting to sense a trap. And by the time he had, it would be too late. He smiled grimly at the pleasure he would derive from placing the manacles on the bastard's wrists.

Sir saw the cold smile on Drew's lips and wondered if the time had come to pull him out of the investigation. It was obvious he was personally involved with Lady Melanie, and he had already learned at a terrible cost what came of mixing emotion with espionage. The pretty little French aristocrat who he had been so foolish as to fall in love with had betrayed him to the enemy, and he had almost died before he was able to affect his escape.

After that he had vowed never to allow himself or any of his men to become emotionally or romantically involved while on assignment. He had broken that vow in Marchfield's case, and although everything had worked out for the better, he was not so foolish as to think it might happen again. If Merrick was so in love with Lady Melanie that he would put her safety above the safety of the mission, then he would have no qualms about replacing him.

"Actually, I should think the earl and his daughter are already amply protected," Sir drawled, his casual tone belying the sharp interest in his blue eyes. "From what you have told me, the marchio-

183

ness and that companion make a formidable team. If you like, we can arrange to have them followed when the earl and the others dine at Carlton House. Lord knows the marchioness is almost old enough to be one of Prinny's flirts."

"That's a thought." Despite the seriousness of the matter, Drew chuckled softly. "She could certainly lead His Highness on a merry chase." Then as abruptly as it came, his light mood turned grim. "Are you quite certain they will be safe?"

"As certain as one can ever be in this business," Sir replied bluntly. "There are no guarantees, Merrick, you know that. And what of you? Will *you* be all right?"

Drew considered the question, knowing Sir would pull him from the mission without a moment's hesitation if he thought him incapable of carrying it through. In the end, however, he knew he had no choice but to do his duty. Not just for his own sake, or even England's, but because it was the only way he could think of to protect his beloved. Until Barrymore was safely locked up, he would not rest.

"I will be fine, Sir," he answered, his voice cool as he met Sir's assessing gaze. "You may depend on me."

Sir hesitated, reading Drew's determined expression before reaching his own conclusion. "Very well, Merrick," he said softly, "then we shall let matters stand as they are. By this time tomorrow evening, it will all be over."

"Yes, Sir," Drew agreed, fighting off a black wave of despair. "It will all be over."

"But, Grandmother, you cannot possibly want to stay home this evening!" Melanie exclaimed, staring at Lady Abbington in dismay. "The prince is expecting us! Whatever shall I tell him?"

"You may tell him anything you demmed well please," the marchioness retorted, pulling the bedcovers up to her chin. "I have the ague, and I'm not stirring from this bed."

Melanie eyed the elderly lady suspiciously, wondering what she should do. To the best of her knowledge, her grandmother had never feigned illness before, and yet she looked rather hardy to be as sick as she claimed. "Are you quite certain you couldn't come just to the dinner?" she asked with a cajoling smile. "I dare say no one would object if you were to make an early evening of it."

"Please, Melanie, the very thought of all that rich French food is enough to make me quite green," Lady Charlotte replied with a shudder. "To say nothing of the stifling heat. One would think Prinny to be as delicate as one of his orchids, as overheated as he keeps Carlton House. No, I would get as sick as a cat, I am sure of it. You and your father go on without us, my dear. It is all for the best."

"Yes, do go on," Miss Evingale urged, assuming a martyred expression. "I shall be more than happy to remain here and bear Her Ladyship company. Pray do not give us another thought."

In the face of such opposition Melanie knew there was little she could do. She could hardly insist that they accompany her without revealing Drew's plans. Besides, she decided, brightening at the thought, given both ladies' love of intrigue, it was probably better for them to remain at home. At least then she needn't worry that they would pop up at some inopportune moment and ruin everything.

"Very well, Grandmother," she said with a heavy

sigh. "If you are so ill, then certainly I won't insist that you accompany us. Would you like me to send for the physician? Perhaps you need a tonic."

"Oh, no." The haste with which she refused the offer convinced Melanie her suspicions were well founded. "I'm not so ill as all that! Besides, you must know that I cannot abide having those simpering quacks poking at me. I'm sure it's just something I ate for luncheon."

"I'm certain that you're right, ma'am," Melanie agreed, secretly wondering what book they were reading that made them so loath to leave. "In that case, I shall leave you to recover. Would you like me to look in on you before we leave?"

"Oh, you needn't bother, for I will probably be fast asleep," Lady Abbington answered, exchanging frantic glances with Miss Evingale. "But mind you keep a sharp eye out tonight, I shall want a full report tomorrow morning!"

After promising to do just that, Melanie gave her grandmother a good-night kiss and went to her own rooms to dress for dinner. In honor of the prince, she had decided to wear the family diamonds, and the precious gems glittered from her ears and throat. She was even wearing the gaudy necklace and tiara that completed the set, and studying her reflection in the glass she thought she looked a perfect cake. Wrinkling her nose in disgust, she picked up the white kid gloves and hurried downstairs, where her father and Mr. Barrymore were waiting.

"Ah, good evening, my dear," the earl said, giving her a paternal smile as she glided into the room. "I am pleased you decided to wear the diamonds; they make you look like a fairy princess."

"Thank you, sir," she replied, smiling as she dipped in a low curtsy. "That is most kind of you."

She turned next to Mr. Barrymore, who was regarding her with admiration. "Good evening, Mr. Barrymore," she said, forcing herself not to recoil from his touch as he swept her hand to his lips, "are you as nervous about this evening as am I? I vow, I fear I shall do something exceedingly foolish and disgrace us all!"

"Never you, my lady," Mr. Barrymore answered earnestly, his blue eyes lingering briefly on the perfectly cut gems circling her throat. "And even if you were to commit some small faux pas, your beauty would more than compensate for any indiscretion. That is a lovely gown."

Melanie accepted his praise with what she hoped was a maidenly blush. The dress was one of Madame Philippe's more inspired creations, and she felt quite exotic in the Nile-blue silk gown with its low décolletage and tiny puff sleeves. When she felt it was safe to do so, she extracted her hand from Barrymore's and told her father of Lady Charlotte's illness.

"Such a pity she won't be accompanying us," the earl said, looking more relieved than disappointed. "But the elderly are often subjected to bodily complaints, so we mustn't be surprised."

"Yes, that is so," Melanie agreed, deciding now was as good a time as any to slip away for a private word with Drew. She knew he was expecting the entire female population of Marchfield House to be at Carlton House, and thought it advisable to inform him of the change in plans.

"If you will excuse me, I believe I shall speak with Mrs. Musgrove," she said quickly. "Even though Grandmother insists she isn't hungry, I want to order a small collation for her. I will be back in just one moment."

As she expected, she found Drew hovering near the door, and after glancing about surreptitiously to make certain they were alone, she hurried to his side. "Grandmother and Miss Evingale aren't coming," she whispered in an urgent voice. "She claims to have the ague, and Miss Evingale is to remain and keep her company."

"I know, Mrs. Musgrove has already warned me," he answered, unable to tear his eyes from her. My God, she was beautiful, he thought, drinking in her appearance hungrily. His fingers trembled with the urge to caress the soft white flesh revealed by the exquisite gown, and it was all he could do to keep from touching her.

"Actually, it all has a rather familiar ring to it," he said, forcing himself to speak in a rational manner. "I seem to recall a particular evening when you remained at home on some pretext of illness."

"Yes, but I don't think you need resort to a pot of Mrs. Musgrove's special milk for them," she replied, her eyes moving wistfully over his muscular figure. He was wearing a butler's coat of black serge and a pair of plain cream breeches, and yet she thought him twice as handsome as Mr. Barrymore, who was dressed to the nines in a jacket of black velvet and white silk evening breeches.

"Do you mean the marchioness is really ill?" Drew asked, his brow wrinkling with concern.

"No, but unless I am much mistaken, she and Miss Evingale will be too busy reading to give you any trouble," she said with a light laugh. "You know how seriously they take their novels."

"Mmm," he agreed, unable to resist brushing a raven-black curl back from her cheek. "But actually I am rather relieved that they have elected to remain here. I must admit I have been in a perfect quake for fear of them stumbling in and ruining our rendezvous. At least here I can keep an eye on them."

"My thoughts exactly." Melanie was pleased their minds were so attuned. "Grandmother does have a penchant for mischief, does she not?"

"Almost as big a penchant as you," he said, his smile vanishing. "Which reminds me, on no account are you to let yourself be alone with Barrymore. I know you are eager to prove your father's innocence, but I don't want you taking any chances."

"I have already given you my word," she reminded him, surprised by the sternness in his voice. "I have read enough Gothics to know that midnight rendezvous are dangerous things; you may rest assured I have no desire to play the heroine."

"I know that, but I also know what a determined minx you can be," Drew snapped, aware that time was slipping inexorably away from him. He wanted to reach out and grab it with both hands, but he knew that could never be. His frustration sought relief in anger, and when he spoke his voice was sharp with displeasure. "I won't have this mission jeopardized by your theatrics, is that understood? Stay out of my way, Melanie. I mean it."

Melanie recoiled in hurt surprise. She had been feeling so close to him, and his unexpected attack brought angry tears to her eyes. Deciding that anger was preferable to the sharp pain she was feeling, she drew herself up to her full height, the top of her head barely reaching his jaw.

"Yes, Davies," she said coolly, "I can see that you do. Allow me to wish you every success in your endeavor, and once it is complete, I hope that I may never see you again!" With that she turned and stormed back to the Duchess's Room, where the others were waiting.

Carlton House was just as hot as Lady Abbington had predicted it would be, and even in her light gown Melanie was uncomfortably warm. The rich food and heavy wines did little to help, and once the supper was over and the gentlemen settled down for port and cigars, she decided to slip out onto the balcony for a quick breath of air. She could see her father deep in conversation with a member of Parliament, but of Barrymore there was no sign.

Earlier she had noted the Portuguese consul general arriving, but Senhor Martinez had not been a member of his party. Later there was such a mad crush of people that she had no hope of finding him. But once the gentlemen rejoined them, she meant to try to seek him out. And Sir, of course, she thought, her lips lifting in a rueful smile. Despite Drew's admonishments that she would never be able to spot his superior, she was determined to prove him wrong.

The thought of Drew brought a somber glow to Melanie's eyes as she recalled the scene in the hallway. What an infuriating devil the man could be, she brooded, leaning against the stone balustrade. One moment he was as passionate and exciting as any hero in a novel, and in the next he was a cold, unfeeling brute. His temper annoyed and mystified her even as his touch made her burn with the sweetest of fires.

She shivered in memory of the kiss they had exchanged last evening. It wasn't that she was a stranger to masculine attentions; at three and twenty she had been embraced by other men. But this was the first time she had ever responded with any degree of enthusiasm. In the past she had always found such embraces distasteful, or, at the very least, disappointing. But when Drew had touched her, held her, she had found herself responding in ways that made her blush to remember.

She gazed up at the stars twinkling in the soft evening sky and thought about the morrow and what it would bring. Her father would be safe, yes, but Drew would be gone. The realization brought a sharp pain that took her breath away, and even as she admitted to the truth behind the pain, she realized she was no longer alone.

"Lady Melanie, I thought I saw you coming out here," Mr. Barrymore said, walking toward her with a cool smile. "I trust you are not feeling unwell? It is uncomfortably warm inside, is it not?"

Melanie whirled around, her heart beginning to pound with fear. All of Drew's warnings were screaming in her head, and she began edging cautiously around him. "Yes, it is rather hot," she agreed, mentally judging the distance between herself and the doorway leading back into the salon. "I was in need of a breath of fresh air, but I am feeling much better now. I had best return before His Highness rejoins the company; it would not do to be late."

"I believe the prince has been detained," Mr. Barrymore said, and something in his silky tones made Melanie's senses sound a clarion warning. "A matter of state, you understand. He will probably not be free for the rest of the evening."

"Well, in that case, perhaps I should find Papa and we can return home," Melanie said with forced brightness. She could hear the sounds of laughter drifting in from the open door, and the knowledge that other people were less than ten feet away filled her with courage. Surely if she cried out someone would come rushing to her aid, she thought, never taking her eyes from Mr. Barrymore as she slid around him.

"I'm afraid I cannot allow that, my lady," Mr. Barrymore replied, pulling a pistol from his pocket and aiming it at her heart. "I suddenly find myself in need of a hostage, and I think you will do quite nicely. No, don't," he warned, cocking the pistol as she opened her mouth to scream, "I have nothing to lose by shooting you or letting you live. I would keep that in mind if I were you."

"You're mad if you think you'll get away with this," she told him, refusing to give way to the fear that was tearing at her. "Drew knows all about you, and he won't rest until he tracks you down."

"Drew?" Mr. Barrymore's dark gold eyebrows wrinkled as if in thought. "Ah, yes, you're referring to our bogus butler, I take it." At her nod he smiled coldly. "Well, my lady, if you are waiting for our gallant young spy to rescue you, I am afraid you are in for a very long wait indeed."

"What do you mean?" Melanie demanded, her fear escalating to an unspeakable terror.

"Merely that the good butler has gone on to . . . shall we say . . . another position?" The evil smile he gave her made Melanie's skin crawl with horror. "He is quite dead, my dear. I killed him shortly after I took care of Senhor Martinez. And now that you realize how very serious I am, I suggest you come with me. Move." He gestured with the gun, leaving a numb Melanie no choice but to follow.

"We've got problems," Sir announced as he came through the servants' door, his face cast in grim lines. "Martinez is dead. One of my men just found him in his room with half his head blown away."

Drew paled at the words. Ever since Melanie and the others had left for Carlton House, he had been strangely restless, consumed by an anxious fear he could not name. He tried telling himself it was excitement over the coming confrontation, not unlike the nervousness he felt before a battle; but he knew it was something far more serious. Something was wrong, he had been sure of it, and now he knew he was right.

"Barrymore?" he asked tersely, already strapping on the deadly-looking sword he had kept hidden in his wardrobe.

"Apparently," Sir agreed, watching as Drew checked his pistol before tucking it in his coat. "He must have seen through Martinez, although God—"

"Gone! Gone! All my lovely jewels!" the marchioness was screeching as she burst into Drew's room, Miss Evingale hot on her heels. "That scoundrel has made off with all of my jewels, and this time I insist that you lock him up!"

"What jewels?" Sir rapped out, glowering down at Lady Charlotte. "Are you talking about Barrymore?"

"Well, of course I am, young man, who else in this household keeps his ill-gotten gain in a hat box, I should like to know?" Lady Abbington shot back, her small jaw thrusting out as she confronted Sir. "The rascal has shabbed off, taking my jewels with him!" She stopped abruptly, seeming to notice only now that the man she was addressing was a total stranger.

"Who the devil are you?" she demanded, shooting him an angry glare. "If you are another Bow

Street runner, allow me to inform you that you run a mighty loose organization! You let that jewel thief waltz out of here with a fortune tucked in his pockets."

"I'll go and check his room," Drew decided, swinging toward the door. "Maybe there's some clue as to where he'll go."

"Well, Portsmouth, of course!" Lady Charlotte snapped, shaking her head at him. "Or at least that's what his valet said before we tied him up."

"You tied his valet up?" Sir echoed, looking slightly green. "May I ask why?"

"Because he was packing," Miss Evingale volunteered, as disappointed as Lady Abbington that two such romantic fellows could be such slow tops. "He says Barrymore is planning to sail on the morning tide, so you really must hurry if you mean to catch him."

"I'll send a rider to alert the navy," Sir said, recovering from the shock to his sensitivities. "What is the name of the ship?" He seemed to take it for granted they would know.

"The *Rose of Redmond*," Lady Charlotte informed him, "and I would have a care if I were you. Barrymore's pistols are also missing, so we can only assume that he took them. Although"—she frowned in disapproval—"it seems a rather odd thing to take to a formal dinner, if you ask me. The prince would never approve."

Drew and Sir exchanged horrified looks.

"Melanie!" Drew groaned, his face paling. "Oh, my God, Melanie!" He turned and ran from the room.

Sir turned to follow, pausing long enough to address the two women. "Guard your prisoner, ladies," he said, the smile he gave them doing much to raise his status in their estimation. "We shall be back for him shortly." And then he dashed out after Andrew.

"Ah, Sir, I rather expected you would be gracing us with your company," His Royal Highness, the Prince of Wales, said, addressing Sir with one of his sweet smiles. "But how disappointing to see you in uniform, as it were. I always so enjoy trying to see through those delightful disguises of yours. You're here about Lady Melanie and our mutual friend, I take it?"

"Yes, Your Highness." Sir was well aware that the prince's affected ways hid a sharp mind. "Have you seen them?"

"Unfortunately I have," the prince sighed, shooting Drew a curious look. "She and Mr. Barrymore slipped out of here not five minutes ago. I am surmising he was holding a gun on her, and so I ordered my men to stand back."

"Which way did they go?" Drew scarcely recognized the harsh voice speaking as his own. All he could think of was Melanie in that madman's hands, a man who had already demonstrated his willingness to kill in the most brutal way imaginable.

"West, with a small contingent of my guards following at a safe distance," Prince George replied soothingly. "A roadblock has already been set up, and they should be reaching it within the half hour. Should he fail to surrender when ordered," he added with the delicacy few credited him for, "I am afraid we will have no other choice but to open fire."

Drew's eyes closed briefly, and when he opened them there was a cold deadliness in them that made the prince shiver with superstitious dread. "He will stop," Drew said softly. "By God, he will stop, or I will personally blast him into hell."

Chapter Thirteen

𝕸elanie had no idea in which direction they were headed, or indeed, how long they had been traveling. Since the moment Barrymore had bragged to her of killing Drew, time had lost all sense of meaning, and she was totally oblivious to what was going on about her. Mr. Barrymore was not so distracted, however, and the farther they went, the more agitated he became.

"That went too smoothly," he decided, peering anxiously out of the coach's window. "We should have been challenged by now. No one can leave a royal residence that easily."

Melanie stirred at his words, trying to think of some sort of response. "We are traveling in my father's coach," she replied, gazing at him with indifference. "Doubtlessly the soldiers recognized his crest and let it pass."

"Perhaps," he conceded, his fingers tapping out a nervous tattoo on his knee. "But I would have liked it better if someone would have at least tried to stop us."

Melanie's lips twisted in a bitter smile at his querulous tones. "Sorry to disappoint you, Mr. Barrymore," she said in a mockingly sweet voice. "Would you like to order the coachman to turn around and try it again?"

Mr. Barrymore's face darkened in anger. "I would watch that saucy tongue of yours if I were you, bitch," he warned her coldly. "You forget you are quite at my mercy, and I can do anything I damn well please to you."

Melanie's chin came up at his insolent words. The numb pain had receded enough to allow other emotions to seep in, and she was overcome with a rage stronger than anything she had ever experienced. If it was the last thing she did on this earth, she vowed, she would see him dead for what he had done to Drew.

"What? No clever comeback such as 'I would die sooner than let you touch me'?" he mocked, his handsome looks completely distorted by the hatred twisting his features. "You disappoint me, Lady Melanie. And here I was so looking forward to taking you down a peg."

"If I were to answer you, it would be to say that I would kill you sooner than allow you to touch me," she replied, deciding the time had come to stop cowering like a Bath miss. "You are a traitor and a murderer."

"You forgot to add bastard," he said, amused by her bold defiance. "For I am that as well as all the other names you have called me. Not that it matters, of course, in a few short hours I will be sailing for the Indies, and if you make a pleasant enough traveling companion between here and Portsmouth, my dear, I may even decide to take you with me." He reached out a hand to touch her cheek, and she promptly slapped it away.

"Ah, that is more like it, my dear Lady Melanie," he laughed, settling back against the squabs of the coach. "Defiance is always much more exciting in a woman than placidness. My mother was as placid as a cow, and look where it got her: a life of shame and then a shallow grave in Potter's Field. But not for me, Lady Melanie, not for me. This time it is *I* who will make them dance to my tune!"

"Them?" Melanie asked, her ears catching the unmistakable sound of a horse's neigh in the distance. It could be nothing, but then again it could be Sir. She wondered if Barrymore was aware of Drew's superior, and prayed that he was not. Her only hope for now was to keep her captor distracted long enough for Sir or whoever was following them to get into position.

"Them, Lady Melanie." Barrymore gave no indication he had heard the noise. "Those lovely people in your world who throw around such terms as *whore* and *bastard* with very little regard for the people whom they are addressing. But I have taught them; my esteemed father has paid dearly for what he did to my mother, and by the time I am finished, my beloved half brother will have paid an even greater price. Why do you think I have been playing such a long and tedious game with your father?"

"I would hardly call treason a game, Mr. Barrymore," she said coldly, wondering if she should make a grab for the pistol he was holding in a casual grip. "And even if it were, I would say it was one you played rather poorly, considering how easily you were caught."

Rather than taking offense at her words, he merely smiled. "Ah, but that was also part of the game, dear Lady Melanie. I knew that once I was suspected, it wouldn't be long until the trail led back to my father and his incompetent son. Why do you think I took that particular dispatch? It was the only document I could find that was sensitive enough and that could be eventually traced back to them."

"Then why did you use my father to cover your deeds if getting caught was your objective? You must have known he would be suspected," Melanie demanded crossly. Had the driver slowed down? It seemed to her the carriage wasn't bouncing about nearly as much as it had been.

"Actually, getting caught was never my objective, but as it was a distinct possibility, I decided I would use it to my best advantage," he answered, shifting restlessly on his padded bench. "As to your father being suspected, that was merely a delightful happenstance. It had never occurred to me an earl would be accused over a mere clerk, but I had underestimated my father's determination to protect Parkinson. He knew if I were caught I'd be damned sure to implicate them as well."

"Then all of this has been a sham? You never intended selling those secrets to the French?" They were definitely slowing down, she realized, tensing in readiness. When the coach stopped she was determined to make a leap for safety, regardless of the danger. Drew had given his life to stop Barrymore, and she refused to allow herself to be used to secure his freedom.

"But of course I did." Again that evil smile flashed. "And they paid for them in good English gold. I told you, no man is averse to lining his pockets whenever the opportunity presents itself. Take those lovely jewels you are wearing"—he indicated them with the muzzle of the pistol—"they will keep me in style for a great many years to come. How thoughtful of you to bring them along."

She sniffed loudly, not deigning to answer the boastful words. Her mind was already spinning with plans of what she would do to Barrymore once she had escaped. He would pay, she vowed silently, blinking back tears of anguish. He would pay for killing the man she loved.

Suddenly the carriage lurched to a halt, and a stentorian voice called out from ahead of them. "You there in the coach, surrender in the name of the king!"

This was her chance, Melanie thought, and then leapt toward the door. She was quick, but not quite quick enough, and even as her fingers were closing around the door's handle, Mr. Barrymore was grabbing her.

"Oh, no, you don't," he said, controlling her struggles with brutal force. "You're my passage out of here, and if I die, then so do you!"

Melanie kept fighting. She had nothing to live for, she told herself, trying to maneuver into a position where she could kick Barrymore in a place that would do the most good. He saw the blow coming and backhanded her, the blow temporarily stunning her.

"That was your last warning," he rasped out, striking her a second time for good measure. "Defy me again and you die." He pushed open the carriage door with his shoulder, dragging a limp Melanie out with him.

"Stand back!" he called out to the contingent of

soldiers who stood blocking the road. "If you come any closer, I will kill her!"

The soldiers hesitated, shooting the hard-faced captain who was their commanding officer uncertain looks. The young officer was equally confused. His orders were to stop the carriage at any price, but no one had told him that price could be the life of the young lady who was standing with a gun pressed to her temple. "What guarantee do I have that you will release her if I let you pass?" he asked, playing for time as he tried to decide what he should do.

"Why, my word as a gentleman, of course," Barrymore mocked, cocking the pistol and pressing the muzzle even harder against Melanie's head. "You have exactly one minute to decide and then I will shoot her."

"Don't listen to him," Melanie said, fighting against the swirling blackness that threatened to engulf her. "He has already killed two men, and he'll kill me once we are away from here. You must open fire."

Such bravery in so tiny a female made the captain even more uneasy. How could he order his men to shoot when doing so would result in her death? As he was wrestling with this dilemma, a second group of soldiers came thundering up behind them, two men dressed in jackets and breeches leaping to the ground and running up to join them.

Melanie almost swooned when she recognized Drew. He was alive, she thought exultantly, and in that moment she was determined to live. Barrymore was distracted by their arrival, and she knew she would never have another chance. Sending a small prayer winging heavenward, she lashed out with her foot and threw herself sideways at the same time. There was a roaring sound that filled her ears and then a flash of pain, and then her entire world went black.

"Merrick, it is time we were going. The doctor says that Lady Melanie will likely sleep for the rest of the evening, and you can do her no good here."

Melanie could hear a voice that sounded vaguely familiar, but as she had a dreadful headache, she decided to ignore it in the hope the speaker would grow bored and leave. She simply wasn't up to company at the moment.

"She would have died out there." A second voice was speaking. "You heard what Captain Edwards said; she told them to open fire."

"An act of exceptional bravery," the first voice agreed soothingly. "But we really must leave now, the prince is awaiting our report. Come, Drew, our job is done now."

Drew! Melanie's eyelashes fluttered frantically as she struggled to throw off the heavy blanket of sleep that covered her. He was leaving, and it was vital that she speak to him. It took a great effort, but she finally managed to open her eyes.

"Drew?" she whispered hoarsely, scarce recognizing the man who was bending over her. His light brown hair was disheveled, and his hazel eyes were glittering out of a face that was alarmingly pale. "You're alive?" she asked, all the terror she had gone through that evening washing over her as she reached up a trembling hand to touch his lips. "He told me he had killed you."

"And I thought he had killed you," Drew said, blinking back scalding tears. The vision of her lying on the ground with blood seeping from her head

203

was an image he knew he would take to the grave. "Are you all right? The physician said the bullet barely grazed you, but that the concussion knocked you unconscious. You should be fine in a day or so."

"Barrymore?" she asked, her soft voice slurring as the blackness began descending again. "You didn't let him escape, did you?"

"He is in custody," Drew assured her, his mouth thinning in an angry line as he remembered the effort it had cost him not to throttle the life from the other man. Had it not been for Sir and the soldiers, he knew he would have killed Barrymore with his bare hands.

It was getting harder and harder to stay awake, and just as she was surrendering to the darkness Melanie spoke the words she had been longing to say.

"Davies?"

"Yes, Lady Melanie?" Drew reached out to brush back a strand of black hair that had fallen across the bandage covering her head.

"I love you."

Melanie spent the next two days abed recovering her strength and fighting off her grandmother's attempts to cure her. She had already spoken with Sir, and once she had his permission, she told her father all that she knew of Barrymore. He was deeply saddened at the calculating way the other man had betrayed him, and vowed to vet his assistants with better care in the future.

Melanie was slowly recovering her strength, but there was one thing that troubled her deeply, and that was that she had neither seen nor heard from Drew. With Barrymore's capture he had vanished completely, and the Marchfields' butler, Mr. Halvey, was now back in his old position. He was a regular martinet, according to Lady Charlotte, who kept Melanie filled in on all that was going on in the household, and far more believable as a butler than was Davies.

"I still haven't forgiven you for spinning me that Banbury tale about his being a runner," she concluded, shooting Melanie a sulky look. "Did you think I would go running off to the enemy with the information?"

"Of course not, Grandmother," Melanie replied quietly, too exhausted to argue with the strong-willed marchioness. "But you must know that I was sworn to secrecy." She turned her head restlessly on the pillows, blinking at the soft golden light streaming into the room through the open drapes. Even as she enjoyed the warm sunshine caressing her cheeks, she realized she had never felt less springlike in all her life. Where the devil was Drew, she brooded angrily. Why hadn't he made the slightest effort to see her?

"Well, if you say so, but I still do not like it," Lady Charlotte grumbled, oblivious to her granddaughter's dark mood. "The very next time you find yourself involved with spies and traitors, I want you to come to me at once! That Davies had no right dragging you into this hornets' nest, and so I told him. Such things are—"

"You have seen Davies?" Melanie interrupted, pushing herself up against the pillows. "He has been here?"

"Well, of course he has," the marchioness blinked at Melanie in surprise. "He has been all but haunting the parlor, he and that blue-eyed devil who is with him. Sir, what sort of name is that? Sir who, I should very much like to know! Although he does look somewhat familiar now that I think of it," she added with a thoughtful frown.

"Why was I not told?" Melanie pushed her bed-clothes aside, fighting off dizziness as she struggled to her feet. Her nightrobe was lying on a chair, and she snatched it up.

"What on earth do you think you are doing?" Lady Abbington gasped in horror, her arms going about Melanie. "Get back into that bed before you collapse!"

Since she was still so weak, Melanie had no choice but to comply, but the moment she was in bed she was issuing instructions. "I want to see him, Grandmother, please ask him to come up here and visit with me."

"What? Entertain a man in your bedchamber? I should say not, young lady!" Her grandmother was clearly horrified. "Your father would never allow such a thing, and even if he did, I would not! We have been lucky enough to scrape through this without a scandal, and I'll not let you risk one now."

"But I want to see him, Grandmother," Melanie insisted, tears pooling in her violet eyes. "Please, can you not arrange it somehow?"

The marchioness studied her for a long moment, and then broke into a wide grin. "Like that, is it?" she asked, sounding oddly satisfied. "Well, never fear, my dear, Edwina and I will take care of every-thing. No, there's no need to thank me," she said when Melanie gasped in protest, "it is my duty as your grandmother to see you leg-shackled, and al-though I think you could do better than an itiner-ate spy, I'll not say a word in protest. Good day, my dear, and be sure to get plenty of rest. Weddings are notoriously taxing on brides." With that she left the room, ignoring Melanie's cries that she come back.

In Sir's rooms Drew sat with his feet up, staring at the contents of his brandy glass. He had just come from a meeting at Carlton House, and the prince's effusive praises were still ringing loudly in his ears.

"You don't look like a man who has just completed a dangerous and difficult assignment," Sir said casually, swinging a booted foot as he studied his friend. "Is there something you neglected to tell His Highness?"

"No, at least nothing that involves Barrymore," Drew replied, taking a deep sip of the fiery brandy. His face screwed up at the brassy taste. "Good God, Sir, I admire your patriotic sentiments, but surely there can be no harm in buying an occasional bottle of French brandy. This bilge water could melt iron!"

"I never, ever buy smuggled brandy," Sir informed him icily, remembering the men he had commanded who had been killed with weapons traded for brandy. "But that isn't the question I asked. Why are you looking so Friday-faced? Has this anything to do with Lady Melanie?"

Drew glared at him. "I told her to stay away from that bastard," he said, stabbing the air with a finger. "I told her he was dangerous. Why the devil couldn't she have obeyed me just this once? She might have been killed!"

"According to what the prince said, it was Barrymore who followed her out onto the balcony rather than the other way around," Sir reminded him coolly, unperturbed by Drew's sullen temper. "You can hardly blame her for what happened."

"Oh, yes, I can," Drew snarled, taking another

sip of the potent liquor. "She is a minx and a menace, and I . . ."

"And you love her," Sir finished when Drew could not continue. "Don't you?"

"Yes, for all the good it does me."

"A great deal of good, I should think, considering the lady in question appears to return your affections," Sir replied quietly. "Or are you forgetting she has already confessed as much?"

"I'll never forget it," Drew answered intensely, knowing he would always cherish her soft confession. "But that doesn't change the fact that she is a lady and I am nothing but the younger son of a country squire. She is used to far more than I could ever hope to provide, and besides, what of my work with you? If Melanie and I were to marry and I were to die, what would become of her?"

"Aren't these questions you should be asking of Lady Melanie?" Sir asked with his usual calm. "If she rejects your suit on such trivial concerns, then there is nothing to be done, but I think you owe it to the lady to ask her. Provided, of course, that you really love her."

Drew did not answer, and the silence between them mounted. Just as Drew appeared to reach a conclusion, there was a knock at the door, and Mr. Halvey entered.

"A thousand pardons for intruding upon you, Sir, Captain Merrick" he said, executing one of the deep bows Drew had been at such pains to learn. "But I think it might be advisable for you to come with me. It is Lady Melanie."

"Melanie?" Drew leapt to his feet, the brandy snifter falling from his fingers. "What about her? Is she all right?"

"I fear not, Captain." The butler's grave tones

made Drew's stomach clench with horror. "She appears to have suffered a relapse. The marchioness sent me to fetch a doctor, but I thought I should inform you as well."

Drew was already pulling on the jacket he had discarded only half an hour earlier, his thoughts all on Melanie. Sir was right, if he loved Melanie and she him, then he owed it to each of them to tell her of that love. If she rejected him . . . He grew cold at the thought.

Sir accompanied them back to Marchfield House, an odd light visible in his deep blue eyes. He would glance at Drew occasionally, a slight smile touching his lips, but he kept his own counsel. Soon they were pulling up in front of the house, and the wheels had barely stopped before Drew jumped out and went dashing up the front steps.

"Where is Melanie?" he demanded of the footman who let him in.

"Her ladyship be in her room," the footman answered, gaping at his former superior in amazement. "But she be resting now, and—"

Drew didn't wait for any further explanations, taking the stairs two at a time in his eagerness. He reached her door and threw it open, groaning in anguish at the sight of her lying so still and silent on the bed.

Melanie heard the door hitting the wall and felt herself being gathered up in a protective embrace. "Melanie, sweet, be all right, please be all right," she heard a soft voice pleading as a string of frantic kisses was trailed across her cheek and down her neck.

She kept her eyes shut, threading her fingers through his thick hair and reveling in the sweet sensations. If this was part of the dream she had been having, then she hoped she never awakened. She sighed deeply, using her hold on her dream-lover to bring his lips down to hers. The ardent kiss they exchanged brought all her senses flaming to life, but it wasn't until she felt his warm hand gently cupping her breast that her eyes flew open.

"Drew!"

"I love you, Melanie," he was whispering, his voice husky with passion as he held her against him. "Please say you will marry me!"

Melanie's eyes filled with tears as she gazed up at him. This was real, she realized, happiness chasing out the last of her bleak despair. Drew was here holding her and speaking the words she had been longing to hear. She touched his cheek lovingly, her voice not quite steady as she answered him. "Oh, yes, Drew, my darling," she said softly, "yes, I will marry you!"

"Darling!" Drew held her close, pouring all of his love and his passion into a burning kiss. When he pulled back, they were both breathing heavily, and Melanie's cheeks were tinted a rosy red.

"The doctor will be delighted to see such color in your cheeks, my love," he laughed huskily, brushing a thumb over the full mouth that was still throbbing from his kiss. "Although he will doubtlessly think himself ill used to have been called out for nothing."

"What on earth are you talking about?" Melanie asked, feeling warm and dazed all at the same time. She wasn't sure why Drew had stopped kissing her, but she wished he would get back to the matter at hand.

"Your head," Drew answered, frowning as he touched the bandage that covered her wound. Gazing down at her, he realized she looked rather healthy for a young lady who was supposedly at death's door. "Halvey said you had had a relapse and he has gone to fetch the doctor."

"But I am fine," she answered, as puzzled as he by the odd circumstances. "When the doctor was here this morning he said I should be up and about by the end of the week."

"But—"

"Well, are you going to stand there all day arguing, or are you going to get properly engaged?" the marchioness demanded, standing in the doorway, her arms folded across her bosom. She wasn't alone; Miss Evingale was standing beside her, a smile of delight lighting her prim face. Sir stood on the other side of her, his eyes sparkling with amusement as he studied the two young lovers.

"I am afraid her ladyship is quite right," he drawled, "after what we have witnessed, I am afraid the two of you really have no course other than to marry. You have been most thoroughly compromised, I promise you."

Melanie and Drew looked at their unexpected visitors and then at each other before breaking into laughter. *"The Romance of Lady Clarice,"* Melanie said as Drew helped her into her dressing gown. "Really, Lady Charlotte, I might have known you would pull such a trick!"

"And don't forget that Gothic nonsense about the relapse," Sir pointed out, enjoying his friend's discomfiture immensely. "I spied that at once, having recently read it in a book. 'The Purloined Heart,' I believe it was called."

"A Heart Purloined," Lady Charlotte corrected him, beaming at Sir in approval. "I am glad to see you took my advice and read it. Did I not tell you such books were instructive?"

"Indeed you did, your ladyship, and if I ever find myself fighting spirits or digging for buried gold, I shall know just what to do. But in the meanwhile, what of our lovebirds? Are you certain the earl will not object to Merrick's suit?"

"Of course not!" The marchioness gave a loud snort. "Percy may be a bit of a stickler about some things, but I assure you he is not beyond all sensibility. Young Drew has proven himself more than worthy of our Melanie, and so long as she loves him, the earl will have no objection. Besides," she added shrewdly, "at the gel's advanced age, we cannot afford to be so choosy. We do not want her to end her days as an old maid."

Melanie knew she should protest, but in truth she was simply too happy to care. Her wildest dreams had come true, and she did not give a whit how or why this had come to pass. She and Drew loved each other, and in her mind that was all that mattered.

Drew shared her indifference at how easily they had been maneuvered by the wily marchioness. He knew he would still have to speak to the earl, but so long as he knew Melanie loved and wanted him, he could face the coming interview with equanimity. Oblivious to the others, he took Melanie's hand and carried it to his lips for a soft kiss.

"Well, I suppose I had best go and talk to the earl," Lady Charlotte said, drawing her tiny frame erect. "I dare say he has worn a hole in the carpet by now. As for you, young man"—she gave Drew a warning glare—"you have five minutes in which to pop the question. Mind you do it properly."

Once they were alone again, Drew grinned down at Melanie. "If either of us had an ounce of pride, we would refuse to get married, if only on general principle," he said, his hazel eyes bright with love. "Not that it would do us any good, I fear. As Sir said, we have been most thoroughly compromised."

"So we have been." Melanie was surprisingly happy about the matter. "If you were to cry off, Father would have to call you out, and only think of the scandal *that* would cause. I am certain Sir would never stand for such a thing."

"Not for one moment," Drew agreed, unable to resist depositing another kiss on her saucy mouth. "He has a positive mania when it comes to secrecy, and he insists that his agents keep as low a profile as possible. He would want me to marry you, if only for that reason."

"Then I suppose we had best post the banns at once," Melanie said, her violet eyes sparkling with warm laughter as she gazed up at him. "If our engagement is long enough, I suppose one of us could back out gracefully without too great a scan—"

His ardent kiss stopped the rest of her protest, and when he drew back she was trembling with desire. "I love you, Melanie," he said, his voice deep with love. "And if you do not agree to marry me, I vow I will carry you off to Gretna Green!"

"Are you quite certain, Drew?" she asked shyly, scarce able to believe in her good fortune. "I couldn't abide it if you were ever to have any regrets. I know I am not the easiest person to get along with. Papa says I have a temper like a fishwife, and I am afraid I am rather managing, and—"

Again she was silenced by his kiss, and when he lifted his head this time, she was more than convinced of his eagerness to become her groom. "I am certain, my darling," he told her quietly. "I love you passionately; and although I cannot say that it may not cause us problems in the future, I must admit that I love your temper and your managing ways. But are *you* certain you wish to marry me? I have neither title nor fortune, and I am involved in work that could take me from your side without a moment's notice. It is difficult, dangerous work, and the time could come when I don't return from a mission. You must accept that, if you accept me."

"Then I accept it all," she said softly, pressing a loving kiss on his tanned throat. She knew living with his chosen profession would be hard, but how much harder was the prospect of living without him. Somehow, she knew they would find the strength to face the future together. Holding back her tears, she sent him a teasing smile.

"And now, Davies, hadn't you best get about your duties? If you remember correctly, my grandmother left you some explicit directions, and I must insist that you carry them out. I intend to be a rather demanding employer, you see," she added, trailing a daring finger down his cheek.

"Indeed I do, your ladyship," Drew replied, drawing her into his arms. "How fortunate for you that I am such a dutiful employee. I shall make it my personal duty to see that all of your demands are most thoroughly satisfied." And with that he gave her a passionate kiss, showing her in a most delightful manner just how dutiful he intended to be.

Regency Romance
at its finest...

MARION CHESNEY